STAR OF THE EAST

Cover design by 17 Studio Book Design

ISBN 978-0-9911893-9-7

Conor McBride International Mystery Series
Deceptive Cadence
The Secret Chord
City of a Thousand Spies

Conor McBride's Family Chronicles
Where a Wave Meets the Shore

Non-Fiction
Five Walks Through Montpelier

STAR OF THE EAST

KATHRYN GUARE

CONOR MCBRIDE INTERNATIONAL MYSTERY SERIES

You see, Watson, our little deductions have suddenly assumed a much more important and less innocent aspect. Here is the stone; the stone came from the goose, and the goose came from Mr. Henry Baker.... So now we must set ourselves very seriously to finding this gentleman and ascertaining what part he has played in this little mystery.

—*Sherlock Holmes and the Adventure of the Blue Carbuncle* by Sir Arthur Conan Doyle

UNTIL HE SAW the body in the middle of the road, Conor had been thinking he was having an excellent night.

Considering it involved food, music, and a stretch of dedicated time with the woman he loved, he ordinarily would assume excellence was guaranteed, but tonight was different. He and Kate had gone nowhere together in months. That wasn't unusual, since it was the inn's busiest season, but this particular evening—a "date night" she'd called it—had an aura of anxiety that felt unfamiliar. For many reasons, they'd badly needed it to go well, and to his great relief, it had.

They'd started with an exquisite fireside dinner at the Rabbit Hill Inn, followed by a holiday concert in St. Johnsbury, and now the drive home over the back roads of Vermont's Northeast Kingdom was offering its own touch of magic. A snowstorm in slow motion had formed in front of the headlights; its lazy cascade fell like icing sugar on the surrounding evergreens.

"It feels like we're inside a snow globe," Kate said.

Her voice had a breathy quality he recognized; it usually meant she was drifting off to sleep. Conor briefly shifted his attention from the road to look at her. Her face, turned to the side window, was obscured by a long curl of auburn hair. As if feeling his glance, she turned, meeting his eyes with the sort of smile he also recognized, and Conor relaxed.

As a man of thirty-three engaged to be married, the words "date night" had conjured the kind of experience he preferred to leave in his youthful past—angst-filled events fueled by liquor, nerves, and confounding mood swings. He hoped they need never use the term again, but her smile, with its implied promise, gave him a greater respect for the underlying concept.

As the truck rolled in silence through deepening powder, leaving a chevron pattern of tire treads behind it, Kate lifted his hand from the gearshift, guiding it to her leg. Trying to keep his focus on the road, Conor felt the stir of something a bit more than Christmas spirit, but then—

"What the bloody hell?"

The snow-covered lump appeared in his headlights like an apparition. Conor stepped hard on the brake, an instinctive reaction but a mistake.

His shout, and the sudden lurch against her seat belt, brought Kate fully awake. She clutched the grab handle above her head.

"My God, what is that?"

"Haven't a clue," Conor said, which was a lie. He'd already assumed the worst.

The truck swerved from the body-shaped thing ahead of them, only to slide toward the edge of the road and the culvert below it. Careful not to overcorrect the first error, he steered out of the skid with only inches to spare. The truck fishtailed away from the culvert and stopped at last, its lights trained on the large, half-obscured mound a few feet away.

"Thanks be to God. It's only a deer." Conor laughed, relaxing his grip on the wheel.

"*Only* a deer?" Kate exclaimed. "The poor thing. How is this funny?"

"It's not, unless you consider what I'd been thinking it was."

"Oh." Kate looked at him, startled. "Wouldn't that have been just our luck."

"Indeed." He flipped on the high beams and popped the door handle.

"What are you doing?"

"I'm going to pull it off the road before it kills someone—a few more minutes and no one will see it under the snow."

With the engine still running, they both exited the truck. Although the deer was almost certainly dead, Conor approached it cautiously, and Kate remained at a distance as he squatted next to the animal.

"It's a two-point buck," he called to her. "Maybe three or four years old."

"How do you know that?" Kate sounded surprised.

"Longchamp's."

She laughed, and he swiveled to grin back at her. "I've learned more than I realized."

In fact, his education in Vermont's rural traditions had been quite thorough, and always entertaining. The regulars at Longchamp's general store thought there were many things a transplanted Irishman ought to know, including more facts about wild game than he ever expected to need.

He ran a hand over the deer, working his fingers into the stiff, wiry fur, dislodging the encrusted snow. As it fell away, a flash of neon appeared. Taking hold of an antler, he shook it and raised the buck's head from the ground. Surprised by what he saw, Conor dropped it again and sat back on his heels.

"He's been tagged."

Kate came forward and huddled next to him, shivering. "Tagged. What does that mean?"

"It means this deer didn't die in a car accident." He lifted the antler again, revealing a waterproofed orange card threaded through a slit in the buck's ear. Moisture had smeared the name on the tag, but the Conservation ID number was still legible.

"He's been hunted, shot, and tagged. And I'm guessing . . ." Standing and nudging Kate back a few feet, Conor rolled the carcass onto its back, exposing a surgically eviscerated cavity. "Right. Field dressed."

Kate took in a sharp breath. "Isn't deer season over?"

"This is the last weekend. So, some hunter is going to be pretty disappointed. Must have fallen off whatever he was using to haul it."

"Or whatever *she* was using," Kate said, leaning in for a closer look.

"Fair enough. Whichever it is, I'm guessing he or she will come looking for it and would be happy not to find it spread all over the road."

He took a foreleg in one hand, a hind leg in the other, and began pulling. The antlers were small, but the buck was large, and heavy. Conor gave it a powerful tug to get it moving. The deer came off the ground and settled again with a thump. After the third pull, something flew from the hollowed-out carcass. Sweating now, he ignored it and dragged the deer far enough to be safe from any passing traffic. Walking back, he saw Kate had plucked the thing from a patch of bloody snow and was holding it up to the headlights. A flip-top Marlboro box.

Conor eyed it hungrily, pricked by a familiar twinge. He hadn't had a cigarette in over a year, which wasn't long enough to kill the craving for one.

"Don't even think about it," Kate teased. The pack rattled as she held it away from him.

"Doesn't sound much like cigarettes," he said. "What's in it?"

She opened the lid, angling it to the headlights, and peered inside. Eyes widening, Kate tilted the box a bit more, and spilled into her outstretched hand the biggest diamond Conor had ever seen.

He stared at the gem, cupped in her palm like a small, sparkling pear. With a tentative stroke, as if touching something wild and alive, he ran a finger over it.

"Sure it can't be genuine. It must be glass, or—"

"I'm pretty sure it's real," Kate said.

Confident she knew far more about precious jewels than he did, Conor accepted the verdict without argument and drew the obvious conclusion.

"I imagine it's stolen?" Kate said, echoing his thoughts.

He snorted and slapped at his coat, searching for his mobile phone. "A huge diamond in a Marlboro box shoved inside a deer? I can't imagine it's *not* stolen. We'll ring the police and let them decide." He checked the phone's screen and sighed. "When we get home. No signal here."

Kate slipped the gem back into the box and tucked it in her pocket. "What?" She shrugged at Conor's worried frown. "We can't leave it here."

"I suppose not. We shouldn't leave the deer, either, and risk it disappearing. The tag identifies the hunter."

"Couldn't you just pull off the tag?"

"I'd rather not touch it. It's a better surface for fingerprints than the cigarette box, and we've probably already ruined whatever prints might have been on the diamond. Anyway, the deer is evidence, as well."

Conor lifted his head to stare up at a swirling kaleidoscope of flakes. He'd envisioned something different for the grand finale of date night. Shaking the snow from his hair, he started back toward the side of the road.

"You're going to get blood all over your suit," Kate called after him. He shot a rueful glance over his shoulder.

"Won't be the first time."

Chapter Two

SOMETHING between them had slipped out of joint. That's why the evening had been so important.

The source of dislocation was no mystery. Kate's family, and all their money—and by extension, all hers—and Conor's fear that they were manipulating their married life together before it even began. He and Kate could make excuses, or pretend it wasn't there, but both of them knew the tension was real, and it was scaring them.

Conor remembered exactly when the trouble started. They'd planned for a simple Vermont wedding with a small guest list, until the family stormed in with a scheme that soon became a mandate—a destination wedding in Montego Bay, at a resort two of her brothers had recently showered with investment capital. With breathtaking speed and histrionic lies about financial ruin, a combination of brothers and their wives recruited the crucial support of Kate's aristocratic grandmother, which brought the battle to an abrupt end. Both he and Kate adored Sophia. They couldn't bear pitting themselves against her, or revealing how she'd been co-opted by her mercenary grandsons, so they surrendered to the certainty of a daft production unlike anything they would have done on their own.

Since then, when faced with all things wedding related, Conor struggled against a spiraling fight-or-flight instinct. It usually surfaced as impatience or irritation, but on one occasion, it turned into something uglier. The trigger came on a rainy afternoon with the news of an engagement party they had no role in planning, because Kate's father had tacked it on to his annual, black-tie holiday gala.

Conor had huddled with her in the inn's office, staring at her laptop, while the brassy voice of Douglas Chatham squawked from the speakerphone. He'd sat obediently, nodding as she scrolled through the menu and fuming in silence at the annotated agenda, including the moment of the Champagne service—Cristal, of course—when her father would announce his daughter's engagement like a mafia don conferring a blessing.

When the call ended, Conor had vaulted from his chair, unable to contain himself.

"This is an endless, bloody nightmare," he snapped, pacing the room in front of her. "Spreading cash around like snuff at a wake, just to make sure everyone knows he's got it. Where does it all come from?"

Staring at the blank screen of her laptop, Kate shrugged, expressionless. "Hedge funds, I suppose. Whatever that means."

"Hedge funds. My arse. I'd say he's printing it in the basement; and he's the star of it all, anyway, so why do we even have to be there?"

"Why do we have to be at our own engagement party?" She looked up at him, her face still unreadable. "Are you seriously asking me that?"

Conor came to a stop. Head bowed, he glared at the floor. "Don't let's pretend it has anything to do with us, Kate. We're extras in this program, somewhere after the welcome remarks and before Broadway Sue or whoever the hell belts out her holiday set."

He faced her, his voice dropping to a low, accusatory register. "This is going to be your father's show, bought and paid for, just like everything else. His monkeys, his feckin' zoo. You hate it, as well—or at least, that's what you've told me—but you seem happy enough now to go along with it."

With a violence that startled him, Kate slammed down the cover of her laptop. She shoved it across the desk and he caught it like a quarterback fumbling the snap, just saving it from crashing to the floor.

"There. Is that what you wanted? Does it take a tantrum to prove I'm not happy with it, either? My family's wealth, my inheritance, my mother's stupid royal pedigree. Yes, I'm uncomfortable with it, too. That's why I moved to Vermont, for God's sake. I know dealing with them is new for you, and I'm sorry your introduction to the 'zoo' is off to such a rocky start, but it's a little more complicated than you seem to think it is; plus, you knew about this and said you could handle all of it. Now, you can't stop being an asshole about any of it; and I'm tired of feeling as though this is all my fault."

"Kate. Hang on. That's not . . . I didn't say it was—"

"Never mind." She sighed. "I have a lot of work to do. I'm going to my studio." She was through the door and gone before Conor could manage another word.

They got through that crisis before the day had ended. Neither of them wanted to carry it into bed with them, much less into a new day. Apologies were offered, kisses exchanged, and promises made, but it wasn't really behind them. Somewhere in their shared anatomy, something had loosened that was supposed to be tight. Earlier in the week, when Kate floated the suggestion of a date night, Conor had jumped at the idea, whatever she chose to call it.

Now, even as the evening drew to a bizarre conclusion, their relief from the uncomplicated pleasure of simply being with each other confirmed how much they'd needed it.

After Conor wrestled the deer into the truck, they drove home, speculating all the way about the diamond and the hunter, tossing out theories that began seriously but became hilarious as they grew more outlandish. At the inn, they pulled themselves together before going inside. Like teenagers sneaking in after curfew, they crept through the front door and Conor shut it softly behind them. They stood in the wide entrance lobby, lit only by the reflected glow of the Christmas tree lights in the adjacent living room, and spoke in whispers to avoid waking any guests.

"I'll phone the police from the office," he said.

"Okay. I'll go make coffee." Kate circled her arms around his neck and pulled him down for a kiss. "This might sound crazy, but I can't think of a more perfect ending for date night. It's just so . . . *us*. Do you know what I mean?"

"I do. It's *us*, entirely." Conor drew her in close, and when her breath released in a sigh after a longer, deeper kiss—he knew what that meant, too.

The *us* was the place they stood inside that no one else could ever touch or understand. It had seen them through a lot already. If they could hold on to that, everything else would be okay.

She headed for the kitchen, and Conor snapped on the overhead light of the office and crossed to sit at the enormous desk opposite the door. This desk, along with the even larger breakfront behind it, was part of the ancestral legacy gifted to Kate by her grandmother.

Both were Biedermeier originals of satin-finished birch that he assumed had been levered out of some Bavarian castle and shipped across the Atlantic. Big as they were, they were often buried in the whirlwind of clutter that was Kate's trademark, but since she'd begun painting again, she seldom used the office. Dominic Perini, the inn's fastidious and long-serving maître d', had taken over the day-to-day management of the inn, and as a result, the desk's gorgeous leather inlay was now always visible.

After finding a number for the police, Conor prepared a mental brief of the evening's events. In almost every respect, he'd strayed well beyond the usual stereotypes of his Irish heritage. A farmer enjoying a second career as a professional concert violinist while also moonlighting as a secret intelligence operative was well outside the mainstream. Still, he retained a few conventional traits, such as a knack for storytelling and a capacity for chatting up and charming people at will. He'd been drilled in suppressing those instincts for after-action briefings, but his training proved a hindrance once he had a Hartsboro officer on the line taking down the story. His delivery was so clipped and succinct that he soon found the need to repeat it slowly, in stages.

"A deer, you said." The night duty officer's methodical cadence suggested she was capturing the details with pen and paper. "Tagged. Field dressed. Pack of Marlboros."

"Not a pack of Marlboros," Conor said, coaching her along. "A bloody great diamond. In a Marlboro box."

"Huh, okay. With . . . diamond in . . . box. And this deer is whereabouts, Mr. McBride?"

"The deer *was* about a hundred feet past the big culvert on Crooked Bend Road. It's *now* in the back of my truck. The truck is at the Rembrandt Inn on Gibbins Road."

"You're staying there tonight, sir?"

"Every night, in fact. I live here."

The Marlboro box in question sat on the desk in front of him. Impatiently, he tapped his own pen against it, grateful now that it wasn't full of cigarettes. He could smell the coffee brewing in the kitchen, and if it hadn't been for the overnight guests, he would have called out for Kate not to bother. He felt sure there'd be no mobilization of the police that evening. The sergeant eventually confirmed this hunch, promising the chief would come to the inn first thing in the morning.

Since no one else seemed urgently interested, after the call ended Conor made an inspection of the diamond, himself. He tipped it gently out of the box onto the desk. The size and stunning brilliance of it startled him again, but the gem also appeared frosty and impersonal, glittering with secrets but giving up none of them. The box offered a stark contrast. It was the standard red packaging for long-filtered Marlboro 100s. On the back, a patch of the glossy coating had torn away, exposing the fibrous card stock beneath it. On the front, he noticed someone had drawn a "T" in black ink beneath the last "O" in the brand name, as if creating a tiny stick figure.

Conor gazed at it and felt a familiar heat tickle the base of his skull. As usual, he didn't know what it meant, but it almost always turned out to mean something.

Chapter Three

FOR CONOR, "first thing in the morning" meant four thirty; for the Hartsboro police, something different. Before anyone appeared the next day, he had time to milk the cows, plow and sand all the driveways, and practice a holiday medley he'd be playing with the Capital Chamber Orchestra the following week. By eight o'clock, he'd parked himself with the newspaper at the kitchen's stainless steel counter, and was basking in the aroma of bacon.

As she did most mornings, Abigail Perini was cooking his breakfast. He'd already eaten one before she'd arrived, but Chef Abigail—Dominic's wife and the more excitable half of the inn's management team—never thought him properly fed until she'd done it herself. He wasn't about to argue. She had an affectionate but volatile temperament, and he did his best to stay on the right side of it.

After the previous night's storm, the morning was cold but crystal clear, with sunlight pouring through the window above the deep porcelain sink. While Abigail moved from stove to counter with the brisk agility of a master in full command of her environment, Conor entertained her with a narration of the police log from Montpelier's *Times Argus*.

"There was a man riding a bicycle on State Street dressed

entirely in bright pink clothing. A checkbook was lost somewhere between Charlie-O's and Shaw's. A pair of boots was found in the road on Park Street."

"Were they pink?" Abigail asked.

He laughed. "It's not mentioned."

They both turned at the sound of a knock on the kitchen door. A blue-uniformed officer opened it halfway and poked his head through the opening.

"Morning, folks. Sorry to sneak in the back way, but the front looked pretty quiet. Guests off skiing already?"

"Hell no, they're still in bed. College students." Abigail ended with a sniff that spoke volumes.

The officer's quick grin showed he was familiar with what Kate described as "the Perini harrumph."

"I'm looking for Conor McBride," he said, nodding at Conor, who, not reacting fast enough, peaceably allowed Abigail to reply for him.

"Well, you found him." She waved a hand in his direction while pulling a tray of bacon from the oven. "Don't stand there letting all the heat out, Reid. Come inside and eat some bacon."

As he entered, Conor did a quick take on the man, guessing him to be in his early sixties. Tall and solid as a tree trunk. Along with a friendly face that creased easily into a smile, his voice had a slight drawl Conor couldn't place. He also had a loose manner of walking. With each step, his torso seemed to lean back, happy to let the legs get out in front. Behind square, wire-rimmed glasses, a keen-eyed flash told him the chief was sizing him up as well. Conor stood to shake hands as Abigail completed the introductions, and he got a firm but not crushing grip in return.

"How are you, Officer. Chief . . . ehm . . . sir."

"Most everyone just calls me Reid." He smiled, taking a seat on the stool across from him. "Don't stand on ceremony around here. Had an interesting drive home last night, I hear."

Over scrambled eggs and bacon, Conor told the story again, allowing himself a more expansive account this time. After breakfast, he brought Chief Briggs to the inn's office and invited him to take a seat while he unlocked the four-by-two-foot safe. Bolted to the floor in a space once used as a coat closet, it had arrived by very special delivery from London the previous winter. The exterior looked conventional—worn, scuffed, and outdated—but beneath its camouflage the safe offered state-of-the-art security, using a bolt-chambered, two-lock entry system with fingerprint access. Along with the now fabled cigarette box and the cash drawer from the inn's gift shop, it contained a few other items not meant for idle observation—namely, two semiautomatic pistols with extra maga-zines, several passports, and a large canvas bag labeled *HM Diplo-matic Service*. Seeing the police chief's fascination with the safe and its locking mechanism, Conor quickly removed the Marlboro pack, closing the safe before he could ogle its more sensitive contents. He handed the box to the chief, who accepted it without taking his eyes from the safe.

"Serious piece of equipment," Reid said lightly. "You've got a pretty sophisticated surveillance system installed outside, too."

Caught off guard, Conor masked his surprise. The system was indeed sophisticated, designed to be virtually invisible. He opted for a sheepish smile. "Seems a bit paranoid, you're thinking? Sure it might be, I suppose."

"Oh, I wouldn't say that. How does that line go? 'Just because you're paranoid—'"

"'Doesn't mean they aren't after you.'" Conor finished the line while Reid nodded along.

Behind their laughter, Conor noted the heightened curiosity between them, and a hint of mutual recognition.

Moving to the window, Reid spilled the diamond into his hand and held it up to a stream of sunshine. In daylight, the stone seemed even bigger, its interior starburst a mesmerizing implosion receding into infinity.

"Someone will surely be missing this." Reid held it to the window, admiring the sharp-edged facets winking in the sun. "Suppose we get that deer down to the reporting station, find out who the tag belongs to. I can't wait to meet this hunter."

Conor nodded. "Half a minute while I tell Kate. She wants to come along."

Before heading up to their third-floor apartment, he made a detour back to the dining room and through its swinging door into the kitchen. Abigail, rifling through a drawer of utensils, looked up, startled.

"You know this guy? Chief Briggs?" Conor asked.

"Reid? Known him for years. I volunteer with his wife, Gwen, at the food bank on Tuesdays. Why?"

"For a small-town cop, he seems unusually . . . acute. What's his story? He has an odd accent. He's not from here, is he?"

"No, they moved up from Virginia a while back. He's a retired US Marshal."

"A retired *US Marshal?* Oh, for fu—" Conor rolled his eyes. "That's a handy bit of information someone might have passed along to me."

Abigail shrugged and began a fresh, clattering search in a different drawer. "Well, I'm passing it along, now."

"I meant a bit earlier, Abigail, before he arrived on the doorstep to gawp at MI6's fancy security system."

Conor spoke with a sharpness she wasn't used to, and it caught her attention. As one of the few people who knew his full life story, Abigail showed a rare humility for the special trust he'd placed in her, and the discretion it demanded.

"Oh." She closed the drawer, a flush of embarrassment spreading over her face. "I see what you mean, now. Birds of a feather. I wasn't thinking. Stupid of me. I'm sorry."

"Never mind about it," Conor said, quickly backpedaling. Abigail erupting in fury he could manage, but Abigail looking close to tears was unendurable. "Sure we run a business inviting strangers into the house every night, don't we? Why wouldn't we have security? Really, Abigail. Don't worry. I doubt he sees anything in it."

He prevented the waterworks he'd feared, but as he headed upstairs to find Kate, Conor didn't believe his own reassuring words. Chief Briggs had seen plenty and was likely working out the rest in his head. Probably, there would soon be another person in town who knew there was more to him than met the eye. He hoped the retired US Marshal knew how to keep a secret.

Chapter Four

DURING VERMONT'S HUNTING SEASON, the law required hunters to tag their deer with a conservation ID number and bring the carcass to a Fish and Wildlife reporting station within forty-eight hours. In the greater Hartsboro area, this was Longchamp's General Store and Emporium in the center of Hartsboro Bend. Its role in hunting season was only a fraction of the "emporium" features implied in the name. It was an ancient, sprawling barn of a place with original floorboards that creaked and groaned with every step. The often-repeated quip in town was that if Longchamp's didn't have it, you didn't need it.

The proprietor was Kate's best friend, Yvette Longchamp. A petite woman of French-Abenaki heritage, she had a Zen-like temperament Kate valued as a counterweight to her own impulsive nature. When she and Conor rolled up in their truck with the deer on board and Reid Briggs in his squad car behind them, Yvette was sweeping away the snow that had blown onto the store's covered porch. At the sight of them, her curiosity registered as a slight widening of her dark brown eyes.

"Didn't know you'd taken up hunting," she said.

From the way her gaze swung back and forth, it was clear she wasn't sure which of them to address. Pleased, Kate gave Conor a playful nudge.

"See? It's an equal opportunity sport."

Conor smiled. "A sport which neither of us has actually taken up, Yvette, but we're getting a pretty good story out of it. We'll tell it inside, will we? It's freezing out here."

"You know where the coffee is," Yvette said. She opened the door for them, but held Kate back with a question. "Still working on your canvases?"

"Still at it, and the clock is ticking."

Kate's wince was only half-comic. She was preparing three oil paintings for her first gallery show in eight years, and had underestimated the level of panic she would feel about putting her work on public display again. It didn't help that she had to manage a growing list of wedding tasks, along with a groom who'd made it clear he wasn't enjoying the process.

She couldn't really blame him; the wedding had spun completely out of their control. Conor called her brothers "hijackers in tailored suits," and as melodramatic as that sounded, he had a point. It was a fitting description of the maneuvers that turned a private celebration into an elaborate "destination wedding" event. At first, she and Conor had been merely amused, and stunned by their audacity. The anger came once they realized the plan was both serious and deceitful, with no good options for countering it. Faced with the prospect of involving her grandmother in a ruthless tug-of-war, the decision was obvious.

"It'll be fine," Conor sighed one night as they lay in bed, staring at the ceiling. "The reason we didn't elope when we were still in Prague was because it would disappoint your grandmother. So, if she thinks we ought to pike away off to Jamaica, I suppose we shouldn't mind it that much."

"I should have let you talk me into eloping," Kate said. "She's already seen me in a wedding dress, anyway."

"Yeah, I saw the picture, remember? You looked gorgeous."

He reached for her hand, and they fell silent. She knew they were both thinking of a night they could never forget, when Conor's past and her own collided. He'd accepted a folder from his MI6 supervisor, who'd traveled a long way to deliver it, and the photograph inside revealed a truth that shattered each of them, but in very different ways. The fallout had come close to killing them both.

"Your first wedding," Conor said. "In all this time, I've never thought to ask where it was, or what it was like."

"It was at my family's summerhouse on Long Island Sound, and actually . . ." Kate paused, then suddenly laughed. "It was in our backyard, and it was *small*."

He rolled over to her. "Ah, well, feck it then. We should do the opposite. Montego Bay, here we come. Bring on the show."

The scale of it chafed at Conor's genetic revulsion for what he called "showing away," but there was some relief in having the question settled, and they might have been okay if not for the engagement party fiasco.

In a phone call, and in the typically rapid, didactic style that always flustered Kate, her father announced his holiday party would be the perfect venue for the announcement. She'd vaguely agreed without giving it—or Conor's reaction—much thought. They'd made no other plans for a formal announcement, and her father's annual display of gaudy, self-promotional excess was a tedious event they needed to attend, anyway.

She realized now she should have taken a stand against it, against all of it, really, but her nerves had become raw from overuse, and her patience for Conor's *im*patience had dwindled. After an especially ugly argument, she'd decided what the two of them most needed was distraction.

Their night out together, and everything following from it, had been perfect for that, a heaven-sent diversion. In just under thirty-six hours, they would be in New York, presented as a featured attraction in a circus neither of them wanted any part of, but in the meantime, there was nothing like a whopping big diamond flying out of a dead deer to keep their minds on something else.

Kate knew Yvette's casual question about her canvases was not the real reason they were lingering on the porch while the men headed to the coffee station at the back of the store. Ever one for the direct approach, her friend came straight to the point.

"So. How was your night out? Did it work?"

"Yes. It was wonderful," Kate said. "You were absolutely right, and I was wrong. I was sure he'd think having dinner at an inn would be too much like eating at home, but he went for it in a heart-beat, and it was amazing."

She shared the details of their evening and how good it was to forget about everything for a few hours. She finished with a short laugh. "It just didn't end the way we'd expected."

Nodding, Yvette did one of her impassive, slow blinks. "You mean there was no sex?"

"Um, no." Kate smiled. "That's not what I mean." She threw a backhanded wave at the truck and its unusual cargo. "I mean that. I'll leave the storytelling to the master. He'll do it much better than I could."

The master storyteller was happy to oblige, and after Conor delivered the tale again over a round of coffee and donuts, Yvette went to look up the hunter's conservation ID number. She returned from her office a few minutes later, her expression unusually animated.

"T-Dell Dunbar! What the heck is T-Dell doing with a diamond like that?"

"Oh!" Kate turned to Chief Briggs. "T-Dell and Gert Dunbar run a bed-and-breakfast in Craftsbury."

"That's a lucky break," he said. "Are you willing to come along while I pay him a visit? Might look friendlier than just me in the squad car."

"Absolutely," Kate said. "Although I can't imagine T-Dell being mixed up in anything like this."

"He doesn't strike you as a jewel thief?" Conor asked.

She snorted. "Hardly."

"Can't be too sure, though," Reid said, looking thoughtful. "People can surprise you."

"Don't we know it." Conor bit into a donut and winked at her.

Chapter Five

WITH ITS STEEPLED white wooden church, matching clapboard houses, and a charming wooden bandstand, the historic village of Craftsbury was a quintessential Vermont country town. Photogenic in all seasons, the Craftsbury Common and its picket fence border looked enchanting under a fresh blanket of snow. Smooth and pristine, it added to the town's aura of brilliance under the morning sun.

The Dunbar Guest House was an old Victorian on a quiet street leading away from the Common, and, like every other building in town, painted white. It sat back from the road, surrounded by a wide-open space and a long, gently rising hill that a few children were climbing, dragging brightly colored snow tubes behind them.

Reid let Conor and Kate take the lead in the truck, and he remained discreetly in the background as they climbed the steps of a covered porch and approached the front door.

Kate pressed the doorbell, and they waited. Getting no response, she exchanged a glance with Conor, who tried it again, leaving his finger on the thin, yellowed rectangle for several seconds.

A reply finally came as a muffled rumble from one of the upper floors, followed by the heavy thump of feet on the stairs. They watched the door in silence while the descent moved at an oddly irregular pace. Conor brushed his fingers over Kate's and took her hand—a casual gesture, but she recognized the subtle shift to a more "operative" attitude. His features grew still and his posture changed; she could almost feel the muscles adjusting, tightening. Then the knob rattled, and the door swung wide open. It sucked at the surrounding cold, and sent back a swirl of the interior air, which smelled faintly of woodsmoke.

T-Dell Dunbar stood in the doorway wearing a ragged thermal shirt and camouflage pants with suspenders. He was potbellied and red-bearded, with his hair sticking up in every direction and his white-stockinged feet planted wide. She felt Conor relax.

At first, T-Dell gaped in sleepy confusion, but then recognized her. "Kate Fitzpatrick!"

It was her former married name, and though she'd been using her maiden name of Chatham for the past year, she'd stopped correcting anyone who didn't realize it, since it would change again soon enough. Kate gave him her best smile.

"Hi, T-Dell. Sorry to burst in on you like this, but I think we've found something you might have lost."

After a few seconds of uncertainty, the penny dropped. With a loud hoot, he bent forward at the waist, eyes popping. "I'll be damned! My deer? Are you serious? I can't believe it! Did you bring it with you?"

His delight was so genuine that Conor's flat expression softened to a smile. "We did. If you want to pull on a pair of boots and have a look, we've got it out here in the truck."

"I'll be damned!" T-Dell repeated while gazing at him, enraptured.

"I don't think you've met my fiancé yet, T-Dell," Kate said. "This is Conor McBride, and this is Reid Briggs, the Hartsboro police chief."

Reid stepped forward, hand extended. "Congratulations on tagging a fine buck, Mr. Dunbar. It's no wonder you're excited to have him back."

With no hesitation, T-Dell grabbed his hand and then Conor's, and finally Kate's, all the while laughing and pulling on his boots, and shrugging off Conor's suggestion that he might want to add a jacket. When they'd gathered around the truck, he seemed on the verge of happy tears.

"It's the only one I got this year, last day of rifle season. Retraced my route all the way back to the highway, hoping I'd come across it. Finally gave up. Figured I'd never see him again."

Conor angled his head, squinting at T-Dell in the sunlight. "Back to the highway. So, you didn't shoot him anywhere close by."

"Nope. Shot him in Groton Forest. My brother's camp is there. I should have left before the snow started, but we got to celebrating and I didn't start out until almost seven o'clock."

Ready to move the action along, Reid cleared his throat and pulled the Marlboro box from his pocket. "Well now, as happy as I am to reunite the two of you, there's something a bit peculiar about this deer and we need to talk about it." Without further warning, he rolled the diamond into his large palm. His voice assumed a tone of authority as he held it out, almost waving it in the smaller man's face. "Can you tell us anything about this, T-Dell?"

T-Dell stared at the gem, transparently dumbfounded. His initial reaction was the same as Conor's. "Is it real?"

"You're telling me you don't know?" Reid shot back, suddenly in full police mode. Kate and Conor remained silent, but she thought they could both see the target of attack was a soft one, without guile. T-Dell looked puzzled.

"How would I? What's this got to do with my deer?"

Reid slapped the diamond back into the cigarette box and showed it to him. "It was found inside the carcass, and I'd very much like to know how it got there."

"Inside the—" His exclamation died away and T-Dell's shoulders stiffened, then abruptly slumped. "Yeah." He stared at the ground, shaking his head, and exhaled a plume of frosty breath. "Yeah, I think I might know how it got there. Last night . . . well, it was damned strange. I guess you'd better come into the house and I'll tell you about it."

Chapter Six

THE INTERIOR DESIGN of the bed-and-breakfast had the hall-marks of a more feminine taste, no doubt that of T-Dell's wife, Gert. With its Turkish rugs, patterned wallpaper, and expensive-looking antiques, the living room to the left of the front door seemed like something that should be roped off and admired from a distance. Conor thought it looked too decorative to be functional, but the solid marble fireplace on the opposite wall had a bed of bright-red embers inside it, and Reid stood with his back to the warm glow.

The furniture arranged around the fireplace was upholstered in green velvet. Kate took a seat on the sofa, and next to her Conor perched on the edge, prepared for flight in case the wife arrived to chase them into some more appropriate den. T-Dell seemed at ease in the room, padding about in his dirty socks, serving soft drinks. Although it was only ten o'clock, he'd started by offering Coors Light. Conor almost took him up on it, thinking the entertainment promised might be worthy of a morning beer, but he settled for a club soda.

"Gert's gone Christmas shopping with her mother," T-Dell said. He plopped heavily onto one of the ornately scrolled chairs facing the sofa, giving Conor the impression of a family dog, going where he shouldn't once his people left the house. T-Dell looked around at them as if wondering what to do next.

"Whenever you're ready," Reid said. He clasped his hands behind him, like a sentry on duty.

Clearing his throat, T-Dell set his glass of Coke on the mahogany coffee table in front of them. Kate slipped a coaster under it.

"Okay, so here's the story. I left my brother's camp last night around seven, and headed over to the Upper Valley Grill to report the buck. That took some time, with the chitchat and all—a few guys there I hadn't seen in a while. Now, I was already in trouble, since Gert was cheesed off about me being late. I needed to gas up the truck, and got the idea to do it at the P&H truck stop in Wells River and pick her up a couple of pies."

"What sort of pies?" Reid demanded.

"What sort of pies?" T-Dell looked confused by the interruption. "Well, there's all kinds. They're famous for 'em. Blueberry, apple—"

"I'm familiar with P&H." Reid took a breath, and then with a slight smile abandoned the pretense of trying to shake up a suspect. "Sorry, T-Dell. Just wondering what kind you picked up for your wife."

"Oh. She's fond of the pecan. And I got a chocolate cream for the kids. But, before any of that, I was at the gas pumps, and this fella comes up to look at the deer, asking what I shot it with, where I got it. It was sort of funny, because I had an idea he didn't know a damn thing about deer hunting. Seemed like he wanted an excuse to talk."

Conor braced his elbows on his knees, more interested now. "What did he look like?"

"Nothing special. City-looking kind of guy. Gelled-up hair. Maybe twenty-something. Skinny. Not dressed for the weather, neither. Wearing one of those suede jackets the color of baby shit." T-Dell's brow wrinkled. He added the man was a little taller than him, and then apologized. "That's about it. I wasn't paying much attention."

"It's actually an excellent description," Kate said. Nodding his agreement, Reid took a memo pad from his shirt pocket and began jotting notes.

"So anyway," T-Dell continued, "he wants to know where I'm going, and when I say I'm headed up '91 he asks if I can give him a lift. He's supposed to pick up a rig in Quebec and drive it across to Vancouver, but the fella who was bringing him up had called saying he was sick and couldn't make it. I ask if he doesn't have someone else to call, and he looks sort of glum. Says he's tried a few people already, but no luck, and the trucker friend who'd dropped him off wasn't answering." He shrugged. "I felt sorry for the guy, standing there shivering, stranded, looking miserable. I told him I'd get him as far as Craftsbury for the price of a room, if he wanted to stay with us and figure things out in the morning. We shake on it, he says his name is Jimmy, and I tell him to hop in the truck. Next, I went inside to the pie counter and—"

"So, he stayed here last night?" Conor broke in, hoping to speed past the minute details of pies purchased.

"Well—"

"When did he leave?" Reid demanded. His head jerked up from the notebook as somewhere farther back in the house a door slammed, followed by a chorus of animated voices. T-Dell waved a hand at the noise, reassuring them.

"That's just the kids, coming in from sliding. No, he didn't stay here. You're sort of getting ahead of the story," he complained, frowning at Reid.

"T-Dell," Kate said gently, leaning forward. "Can you tell it a little more quickly? We're all but certain the diamond in that box was stolen. We know it wasn't you, but if it was this guy Jimmy, we need to find him."

Conor noted the "we" in her statement, and, catching his raised eyebrow, she confirmed her intentions with a devilish grin. They were in it for the duration.

"Okay, okay." T-Dell shrugged. "There isn't a lot more to tell, anyway. He seemed kind of twitchy when we started out, but settled down after a while. I asked a few questions about driving a tractor trailer and I'll say this for nothing—he didn't know no more about it than he did about deer hunting. Now, that made me a little suspicious. We didn't talk much after that, until we got home and . . . no buck. It was on that curve by the brook, wasn't it?"

He looked at Conor, chuckling when he nodded. "My tires are . . . well . . . kind of bald. We nearly went off the road right there. Like I said, I drove back to the highway exit, but the snow was all rucked up by that curve. I sort of knew that's where I lost it, and that somebody else had it. Easy enough to stick a new tag on it. Jimmy went crazy over it, which at the time just seemed weird. He wanted to keep looking and I finally had to shout at him that I was going home. At that point he changed his mind about staying. Offered me two hundred dollars cash to take him closer to the Canadian border. So I hauled him up to Newport, dropped him at a motel off Route 5, and collected my two hundred bucks. Came home and took a ration of shit from Gert. To be honest, I was glad not to have him in the house, thought maybe he was a druggie or something, but—" He burst into hooting laughter. "I never would have guessed he'd go shoving a diamond up a deer's ass. Must have been while I was in getting the pies. Why the hell did he do that?"

"It's a good question," Conor admitted. "I suppose he was hiding it, but Jaysus, why there?"

"Maybe while T-Dell was inside he panicked for some reason," Kate said.

"Possibly," Reid said. He scribbled a few more notes, and then frowned at T-Dell. "You were there. Think about it. Who was in the parking lot? Or the restaurant? Notice anybody watching the two of you? Anyone drive in while you were talking?"

Responding to the chief's encouragement, T-Dell made a visibly determined effort to remember something useful. He pulled on his lower lip, hummed in thought. "Didn't see anyone suspicious. There weren't many in the parking lot but the restaurant was packed. I didn't notice anything getting the pies, but I wasn't looking for anything at the time. I was in there about ten minutes, came back out, talked a minute with Rob and Edgar, and then we took off."

"Who are they, now?" Conor demanded. "Rob and Edgar?"

"Just a couple of game wardens. I know them. They wouldn't get mixed up in—ohhh." T-Dell's mouth formed a circle as the light dawned. "They were in uniform. Maybe he thought they were cops, looking for him?"

Before Conor could reply, Reid had snapped the notebook shut, zipped his coat and was striding across the room.

"Thank you very much, Mr. Dunbar. I think we've got all we need. Happy to return your deer to you. Be good if you could stay away from that truck for now. Someone will be up before long to take some prints."

"Oh. Well, okay . . ." Flustered, T-Dell stayed in his seat, accepting the quick handshake Reid offered before heading to the door.

Jumping to catch up, Conor and Kate rose from the sofa together, offering their own hurried farewells. T-Dell at last clambered up from his chair to watch them go, looking surprised—and a little disappointed—that the spotlight had moved on so quickly.

Chapter Seven

WHEN THEY REACHED the parking lot next to the house, Chief Briggs was already sitting in his car delivering instructions by phone. Conor was struck by the difference in him. With growing evidence of a crime, his slow, laid-back manner had shifted to brisk professionalism.

"Do you know anything about him?" he asked Kate.

"Not really. I've met him a few times. He and his wife come to the inn for dinner once in a while. Abigail knows them better than I do." She turned to look at him. "Why? Are you getting a vibe about him?"

"No, no. Nothing like that. It's only that she said he's a retired US Marshal from Virginia. I'm wondering what's landed him way up here, in the back of beyond."

"He's probably wondering the same about you."

Conor grimaced. "That's what I'm afraid of. He picked up on the security system, and I was too careless with the safe. That bloody great diplomatic bag is in plain sight and he got an eyeful before I realized he was paying so much attention."

Kate's eyes widened. "How much do you think he's figured out?"

"Maybe not a lot, but I'm betting he'll get there, eventually. He seems like the curious type, and he's fairly sharp."

They talked quietly, leaning against the truck and watching as Reid ended one call and started another.

"He'll be calling in the FBI, I imagine," Conor said. "They must have some sort of unit for high-end jewel theft."

"And this is definitely high-end," Kate said. "It's kind of exciting to be involved, isn't it?"

"We're *involved*, are we?" He shot her a teasing glance.

"Of course. He's going to ask you to help him."

"What makes you think so?"

"Intuition. I'm catching it from you." She reached up to kiss his chin. "You can be his Dr. Watson."

"Rubbish. Why can't I be Sherlock Holmes?"

"Whichever." She laughed. "Don't pretend you're not thinking the same thing—that a little adventure is exactly what we needed." She smiled at him, cheeks pink, blue eyes shining, a few curls of hair straying from beneath her white knit cap.

"Am I right?"

Conor gave the tip of her nose an affectionate tap. "You always are."

Reid had exited the squad car now and was crossing the parking lot toward them, hands tucked in the pockets of his navy-blue duty jacket.

"Couple of things. First thing. Sergeant Fox faxed me the report you phoned in, and I read it last night. I could only assume 'bloody great diamond'"—he grinned at Conor—"meant something either from a museum, an exclusive jeweler, or a private collection. I asked her to sniff out any reports of a theft fitting the profile we've got. So far, nothing. Seems most likely our suspect came up I-91 and I'm guessing he didn't start from Brattleboro, so she'll narrow the focus to the areas farther south around the interstate corridor. She'll also come over and do the fingerprints on T-Dell's truck. Second thing. I updated the State Police. They'll send someone to ask a few more questions at P&H, see if there's anything else to learn there, and they're coordinating with the FBI to get an expert up here to examine the diamond. They asked for a local hotel recommendation—"

"Yes," Kate said, nodding decisively. "We've got plenty of rooms, and they can use the office. I'm sure we have whatever they need."

"Much appreciated. Don't offer any discounts; they can afford the going rate. And, there's one last thing . . ." Reid paused, rubbing his chin. "I'm heading up to Newport to see if I can pick up the trail of young Jimmy. I could use a good wingman." His eyes wandered off to a point beyond Conor's right shoulder. "In the military sense of the term."

Ignoring Kate's jab to his stomach, Conor feigned surprise. "You've a few officers back at the station to call on, surely?"

Reid was still looking at some fascinating bit of sky. "I said a *good* wingman. By which I mean . . . experienced."

Kate jabbed him again.

"*Oof.* Okay, give over." He nodded at the police chief. "Right. Shall I go back to collect the Walther you no doubt ran your eyes over when I opened the safe, or have you got a spare to lend me?"

Grinning, Reid pointed a knowing finger and clapped him on the shoulder. "I don't think we'll be needing that kind of firepower for this one, Conor."

"Yeah, well, don't be too sure," Conor said. "As you said, people can surprise you."

WHENEVER HE TRAVELED any distance along the roads of Vermont, Conor felt as if he kept seeing the same white church every ten or twenty miles. He could nearly believe there was only one, and by some clever bit of wizardry Vermonters moved it around, only to confuse him. On Route 14, he could have sworn he saw it three times as they sped north through Albany, but he couldn't spare much thought about it. The job of wingman included administrative tasks, which meant making phone calls while Reid drove toward Newport.

Cell service was spotty throughout the state—the northeast in particular—but he made the most of his opportunities. Before they reached Irasburg, he was speaking with the owner of the Clyde View Motel on Route 5 in Newport. A man who signed in as "Jim Smith" had indeed paid cash for a one-night stay late the previous evening, and someone named Bevvie had been the overnight staffer on the desk when he left that morning. Bevvie wasn't available, but the owner promised to track her down and call him back. The cell phone buzzed at him a few minutes later. It was Bevvie herself on the line—not a teenaged girl, as Conor had guessed from the name, but an older-sounding woman with a wheezy smoker's voice.

"Yeah, Jim Smith—what a laugh, right? We get these characters sometimes, paying cash, headed for Canada. None of my business, though. He didn't want to rent a car because—credit cards, right? I assumed, anyway. This morning, he took off early, said he was going to walk into town for breakfast and then call a cab."

"A cab?" Conor asked, after briefing Reid on the call. "Is that allowed, then? Taxis into Canada?"

"Sure, they do it all the time. So long as everyone's got their papers, it's fine. Some drivers wouldn't want the hassle, though."

"Right. How many feckin' taxi companies does Newport have, I wonder. Maybe Bevvie will help." Conor punched up the recent calls list and selected the number.

Bevvie picked up immediately. She was happy to help. She'd been telling Christine what a beautiful voice he had. Was it a British accent?

"It is indeed, Bevvie," he lied, troweling out a thick dose of the Kerryman's brogue.

It turned out there were only two taxi companies in Newport, and yes, Bevvie could of course get him the numbers. Calling the first, he learned they had no one who'd driven to Canada, and the operator wondered what was going on up there. Another guy had asked the same question that morning.

He struck it lucky with the second company. Nancy, from Town Taxi, reported one of their drivers had just crossed the border on his way back from Canada. After a few minutes of persuasion, she coughed up the cell phone number for Anthony. By the time the squad car was rolling out of Irasburg, he had him on the line.

"Who is this?" the cab driver demanded, upon answering.

"Is that Anthony? Town Taxi?"

"Who are you?" the voice snapped. "This is a private number."

Conor had a notion it would be unwise to repeat his earlier script—that he was making inquiries from a special unit of the Hartsboro Police Department—"special unit" being the squad car.

"Right, right. Sorry about this," he said, thinking fast. "This is the Clyde View Motel. You've a passenger named Jim with you? He's left his cell phone behind. Will you ever put him on the line, please?"

"He's not here. I dropped him in Magog, half-hour ago."

"Ah, jayz. Where was that, now?" After a few beats of silence he asked again. "Sorry? Where in Magog did you drop him?"

"Parking lot. Company called Vallencourt," the driver said, and then added, "He did have his cell phone with him."

"Did he, so? Bloody hell. Who's have I got, then? Right. Cheers. Byeee."

Conor tossed the phone into the cup holder in the center console. "Ta-daah. Town Taxi Anthony dropped him half an hour ago in the parking lot of a company named Vallencourt, whatever that is."

"Not bad for a few minutes of detective work." Reid smiled without taking his eyes from the road. "I knew I was on to something with you."

"I figured as much. Keep it under your hat," Conor said. "And don't be getting fancy ideas once this is over. I'm completely unreliable. I get frightened and don't know where I am by sundown. And I'm a drunkard. Unsuitable in every way."

Reid laughed, and then grew more serious. "I guess it's a 'need to know' deal, whatever line you're in?"

"You guess correctly." Conor shifted in his seat, uncomfortable with the topic. He pushed his boot against the McDonald's bag on the floor, flattening the empty coffee cup inside it. "It's not really a 'line,' anyway. I'm mostly what you're looking at—farmer, fiddle player, and general assistant to a beautiful innkeeper who's marrying me against her better judgment, no doubt."

"All of that, but a few hidden talents."

"I suppose so, yeah."

He stared out the window at the leafless birch trees lining the road, then swiveled back to study the profile of the police chief. "A few hidden talents much like yourself . . . *Marshal* Briggs."

Reid bowed his head, conceding the point. "Witness security, and special projects at the headquarters in Arlington. Twenty-six years altogether."

"What made you come to Vermont?"

"What made you?"

Conor smiled and looked away. "Fair play."

"Sometimes . . ." Reid stopped, then began again after a long pause. "Sometimes, things just go wrong."

Conor nodded, his eyes fixed on the road ahead of them. "Yeah. Sometimes they do."

Reid abruptly sat up straighter and cleared his throat. "We'll stop in Newport before going any further. I need to make some calls on a decent phone line and put together a plan for the border. What kind of ID are you carrying? Green card?"

Conor relaxed, glad to be back in less personal territory. "Never leave home without it."

"Hmm, not sure if that's going to help or not. An Irishman and a cop show up in a Hartsboro squad car, wanting to track a jewel thief into Canada. That sounds like it will need a few hours of explanation."

"Why would they let us through, anyway?" Conor said. "Vermont cops have no jurisdiction in Canada."

"True enough." Reid's tone was casual. "But US Marshals often work with Canadian counterparts on tracking and extraditing fugitives."

"Ah, I see. Does that mean you're not actually retired?"

"That means I'm not actually retired." Reid glanced over and winked at him. "Keep it under your hat."

Chapter Eight

THE MORNING SUN disappeared behind a wall of cloud as they drove north, and it began snowing as they approached Newport. When they arrived, it looked to Conor like a place winter had swallowed whole. By now, in the second week of December, all of Vermont had experienced some degree of snowfall. In Newport, it seemed as if it had been pelting down for months and hadn't stopped yet. What wasn't in the road was heaped on either side of it in four-foot piles, narrowing the width of the street and making the passage of cars in both directions slow and cautious. The rooftops all had the same, uniformly thick layer of powder, adding several inches to their height.

Reid navigated a slick turn onto Main Street. "Must be lake-effect snow," he said.

"Jaysus, it's quite an effect, all right." Conor stared at the ice-capped scale of the glacial Lake Memphremagog. It was hard to believe most of it was in Canada, but the highway map showed it was only the wider, bottom end that stretched into Vermont. The city of Newport covered both banks, enveloping the lake's southernmost tip in a close embrace.

The snow lent a magical atmosphere to the downtown area, which looked festive and ready for the holidays. Storefronts were trimmed, streetlight poles were wrapped in lights and garlands of evergreen, and the city's residents appeared to be making the most of what was dished out to them. As the car passed a filling station, Conor saw a group of snowmobilers had stopped to gas up their machines. He also noticed a set of ice rinks in the city park, with skaters gliding along the paths that connected them.

At the edge of town, Reid turned off the main road. They drove under a railroad trestle and onto a quiet lane that was even more snow covered. The tires spun before regaining traction.

"When do we get to Grandmother's house?" Conor asked dryly. "I don't think this sleigh will go much farther."

Reid laughed. "We're almost there. There's a pub down here by the lake."

"You're joking me."

"You'll see. It makes more sense in the summer. I need a private office, and I know the manager."

As evidenced by the front door handle styled in the shape of a ship's anchor, the Eastside Pub had a nautical theme, and a long, honey-colored bar polished to a high shine. An expanse of deck hung out over the lake; it indeed looked just the place for a cool summer cocktail. Conor filed the thought away for future reference. It was a little early for lunch, but once inside, he realized detective work made him hungry. While Reid went off to the manager's office, he sat at the bar and ate a bowl of beef barley soup with a side of french fries. By the time his new partner reappeared, Conor was on his second mug of tea, having persuaded the bartender to boil the water to its proper volcanic temperature.

"No Guinness?" Reid joked. "What kind of Irishman are you?"

"The whiskey-drinking kind, but it's too early. How did you make out?"

The police chief pulled a sour face. "Not great. Federal bureaucracy, red tape, blah blah. They told me to call again at noon, but I'm sure our friend Jimmy won't be hanging around a subzero parking lot in Magog by then. He's getting farther away by the minute."

"Uh-huh. We need someone to 'dry the roads' before us, so to speak, is that it?" Conor asked.

"That's the idea, yeah." Reid took a seat at the bar and shot him a loaded glance, but said no more.

Conor drained his mug of tea and nodded. "I'll have a go at it. Will yer man in the office let me do an international call?"

The man would. In fact, the beefy, florid-faced manager was so nonchalant about having a policeman and his sidekick using the phone that Conor suspected it wasn't the first time he'd done this favor. Small and tidy, the office conformed to the same maritime theme as the restaurant—a few decorative brass portholes, a collection of sextants, and everywhere framed photos of proud fishermen displaying their catches. Conor took a seat at the large oak desk. He gazed at a trophy mounted on the opposite wall—the ubiquitous, needle-nosed marlin—before reaching for the phone.

"Right. Let's see if this works."

He felt sure that a call from a number identified as the "Eastside Pub" would never be accepted under ordinary circumstances, but since it was also originating from the state of Vermont, the odds were better. The line nearly did ring out, indicating a certain level of hesitation, but after five repetitions there was an abrupt click, followed by a familiar hiss that told him the connection had not failed. He waited in limbo a full minute, picturing a junior officer in the bowels of Vauxhall Cross debating with himself.

Conor knew some in the British Secret Intelligence Service took a dim view of his part-time, semi-official status, but he'd shown his value on a few occasions now, and the man who'd recruited him was senior enough, and clever enough, to get what he wanted. The current phone call proved no exception. A few longer rings in a lower register signaled its acceptance, and at last he heard the smooth voice of Frank Emmons Murdoch, laced with its usual razor-sharp irony.

"That's the Eastside Pub is it? Where the bloody hell are my sandwiches?"

Conor laughed. "Where should I deliver them?"

"Well, let me see. Dare I to hope, Conor, that you've rung from a secure line?"

"Ehm, no."

"Of course not, but what's the point? Unless Newport, Vermont has blossomed into a hotbed of intrigue, who on earth would be listening?" Frank sighed. "I'm on the Vistula Spit, if you can believe it."

"Where the hell is that? It sounds like a disease."

"It's an overgrown sandbar stretched like a flabby arm between Gdansk and Kaliningrad, and it is in every way the festering sore its name suggests. Outside I smell nothing but rotting seaweed and inside nothing but cabbage. I can't decide which is more revolting."

"Right so. It's a holiday, then."

Frank gave a bark of laughter and then resumed in a more natural tone. "It's a nightmare, but all I can tell you is the weather is appalling and I'm sleeping in a caravan. Now, you sound perfectly healthy, so reassure me that Kate is the same and tell me what the devil is going on in Newport of such singular interest that you've kindly included me in it."

Conor tried to keep it brief but was continually interrupted by incredulous questions and fresh peals of laughter emanating from the Vistula Spit. Frank's extraneous commentary pushed him over the edge as well, and by the time the tale was finished, his own sides were aching. He imagined the manager wondering what sort of sideshow was going on in his office.

"I'm sure I can organize something," Frank said, when they had collected themselves. "They are in the Commonwealth, after all. What did you call it? Derby Line?"

"That's the border crossing, yeah. It's about six miles north of where we are now."

"Right. Well, give me an hour. I don't know who, but someone will be there, and I'll leave them to get the story from you. I couldn't possibly choke it out without roaring again."

"Thanks, Frank. I appreciate it."

"No, thank *you*, my boy. My mood is enormously improved. By the way, Eckhard was asking if perhaps our wedding invitation had gone missing in the mail?"

Conor smiled at this delicately phrased probe. "They aren't in the mail yet. The date is still the seventeenth of April, but there have been a few recent developments. You'll want to be checking flights to Jamaica."

"Jamaica," Frank purred, clearly pleased with this news. "Splendid. I'll jot it down."

Before leaving the manager's office, Conor phoned Kate to let her know the manhunt for Diamond Jimmy was on the verge of becoming an international operation.

"I can't believe you dragged Frank into this," Kate said. Her amusement held a hint of scandalized wonder that he'd gotten away with it. "Was he annoyed?"

"On the contrary, he was grateful for the diversion. So if he's able to get through to someone, we'll be belting off to Magog in hot pursuit. All of which is to say I may be late for dinner, but to be honest I doubt we'll find the guy. It's over an hour since the taxi dumped him in a parking lot. He could be anywhere. What's happening on your end?"

"Someone from the State Police called. There are two agents from the FBI's Jewelry and Gem Theft program on their way. They'll probably be here by the time you get back. Oh, and before I forget . . ." Kate hesitated. "I'm getting your tux ready for tomorrow night and I can't find the bow tie."

"Killjoy," Conor said morosely.

"Don't start!"

He laughed. "I'm only messing. I think it's in one of the pockets."

Chapter Nine

WHEN HE RETURNED to the bar with encouraging news, Reid didn't ask for details, but he seemed impressed, and a little sheepish that a nebulous, international fixer was outshining the US Marshals Service. An hour later, he was giving their names to the Canadian guard at the Derby Line border while Conor held his breath. After an intense frown at their ID cards and a few animated exchanges over his radio, the border guard gave them an impatient wave, directing them through to a covered bay of parking spaces on the left. As he'd promised, Frank had delivered.

Unsure of their instructions, they parked and got out of the car, and then stood waiting for whatever came next.

"Do you speak any French?" Reid asked.

"I thought I did," Conor said, "but I didn't get any of that. It sounded like he was having a stroke."

"Ha! No stroke, it's just the Québecois that you're not used to."

Startled by the voice that seemed to come from nowhere, they turned and saw a tall, plump woman had emerged from the station's office building twenty yards away. She wore a voluminous blue anorak with a regal-looking crest on the shoulder, and on her head, the traditional winter headgear of the Canadian police—a dome-shaped wool hat with flaps pinned up on all sides, displaying a fur-lined interior.

"You have quite a keen sense of hearing," Reid said, as she approached.

"So you better watch what you say, right?" In a crisp, French accent, she shot back the reply with a rapid, staccato rhythm that would have sounded combative if not softened by her laugh. It was a deep, rolling sound that Conor could imagine carrying for miles in the frigid air.

"Our colleagues in London asked that I facilitate your arrival in Canada," she said, briskly taking charge of the introductions. "You must be Deputy Marshal Briggs; or should I call you Chief Briggs?"

"I'd prefer it if you just call me Reid."

"Okay. I will. And, Conor McBride." Her voice dipped as she turned to him, her eyes widening in mock wonder. "My instructions from Ottawa say I am not to know what title you hold."

He smiled. "I've never been told I have one. Conor is fine."

She nodded. "Good, and Nicky will do for me, but to make things complete I am Sergeant Monique Simard of the Royal Canadian Mounted Police." She shook a finger at each of them. "Don't go looking around for horses. No horses are coming." Nicky started back to the station office, beckoning them to follow. "Let's have some coffee, okay? You tell me what you need, and I tell you if I can help."

They gathered at a table in a sterile, white-walled space that wasn't much warmer than the parking lot. The coffee was undrinkable but infused the air with a pleasant aroma, and Conor welcomed the heat of the paper cup while he and Reid presented their case. Perhaps because Quebec and Vermont shared a few cultural traits and hunting traditions, Nicky's response was not the same as Frank's gut-busting hilarity. She found the narrative entertaining but soon dug into the details, which Conor appreciated. In the rush of organizing logistics, they'd spent no time on analysis.

"This fellow, Jimmy, tells a story to get a ride." Nicky underlined one of the bullet points she'd scribbled on a legal pad. "We think it's bullshit. For now, okay? Let's think it's bullshit. How does Jimmy with a diamond in his pocket end up at a truck stop with no truck, no car?"

"Suppose he had one there, but was afraid to drive it?" Conor suggested. "In case a scene-of-crime witness might have identified it?"

"Doubtful," Reid said. "The State Police will check the P&H lot, but it seems foolish to give up his own vehicle to hitch a ride with a stranger."

"Maybe he's not such a smart criminal. But, you're probably right." Nicky put a stroke through the bullet point. "Okay, he got stuck there. That part is not bullshit."

"At least some of the rest of it must be, though," Conor said. "Assuming he got stranded, it's a simple either-or scenario: either he was dropped off and expected to meet someone who never showed, or Jimmy didn't expect to meet anyone because he hadn't meant to be there at all. That would mean someone dumped him and left."

"For both cases," Reid said, "there's at least one other person who knows he was there. A boss, a partner, a buyer." He tapped the table to punctuate each of the possibilities. "Somebody's got a story to tell."

"One we're not likely to hear if we Don't. Find. Jimmy." Conor mimicked the police chief's rhythm with a finger against his wristwatch.

"Okay, okay, Conor McBride! He's in a hurry." Nicky released another laugh that bounced off the empty walls. "We'll go and find him then, no?"

"You'll help us?"

Reid's hopeful question made Conor realize the entire meeting had not only been an explanation of purpose but a petition for assistance. Without the cooperation of the RCMP, they would have no option but to slink back over the border and go home.

"*Mais oui*. Delighted. Your influence with Ottawa is rescuing me from a desk full of paperwork in Sherbrooke. I am your partner and guide, and . . . okay, your chauffeur. You can't chase around

Quebec in a police car from Vermont. No one will pay attention, you see? Just tell me where we are going."

"To a parking lot in Magog," Conor said, explaining that Anthony, the surly taxi driver, had reported dropping Jimmy off at that location near a company called Vallencourt. At the name, Nicky jabbed her pen in his direction.

"Ha! Vallencourt Logistiques."

"You've heard of it?" Reid asked.

"Yes, yes, and I see it, on a weekly basis at least, right here on this very spot." She gave them a broad smile. "Among other things, it is a trucking company."

"Bingo!" Reid bumped his fist against the table. "There's got to be a connection there."

Conor's reaction was more ambivalent. "Maybe the fecker was telling the truth about that. He picked up his rig to head across Canada."

"Maybe," Reid said, "but Vallencourt will have a record of the route he's taking."

Nicky capped her pen and pushed away from the table. "So, we're off to Magog. I'll get the car for us and find the address for Vallencourt's office."

When the door had closed behind her, Conor turned to Reid. "You'll chase him all the way to the Pacific, then? Because I can't sign up for that adventure. Kate and I have a flight to New York in the morning."

"Understood." Reid smiled. "If it starts looking that complicated, we can always call Town Taxi to get you back over the border."

"Yeah." Scowling, Conor pushed the now cold cup of coffee away from him. "Don't think I'm not tempted. A flying visit to Vancouver sounds a picnic compared to what I'll be doing instead."

A few minutes later, Nicky stuck her head through the door. "*Aweille!*" Amused by their confusion, she snapped her fingers. "Québecois, my friends. It means 'move your butts.'"

❄

MAGOG WAS a half-hour north of the border. In between, there was just a conifer-lined stretch of road with two lanes, straight and flat. Within the space of a few miles, Conor saw two herds of deer sauntering next to it, ignoring the RCMP's Crown Victoria as it sped past.

When they arrived, his first impression was that Magog resembled Newport, but in the way rich people might share a likeness with their less prosperous relatives. It had the same picturesque setting on the same lake, with a mixture of old and new architecture, and at least as much snow with plenty of outdoor enthusiasts taking advantage of it; but the city was larger than Newport in both area and population, and it seemed to have more going on—more shopping, more restaurants—and, of course, all the signs were in French. Many of them advertised the annual opening of the *sentier glacé*, which Nicky explained was a skating trail, a glistening ribbon of ice along the shoreline of the lake.

"Magog is a shorthand reference to the lake, I suppose?" Conor sat forward, speaking through an opening in the car's acrylic shield. He'd volunteered for the "perp" seat in the back so she and Reid could swap police stories.

"Most people think so," she said. "It's an Abenaki word, *Memphremagog*."

"Meaning?" Conor asked.

"Big lake."

"Ah, brilliant. Very practical."

Nicky steered away from the shopping district. She drove through a more industrial area then turned down a road near the railroad tracks that dead-ended at Vallencourt Logistiques in an unexpectedly rural setting, edged by the beginnings of a forest on one side and the north bank of Magog's winding river on another. The building was cornflower blue and looked to be constructed from the same corrugated steel used to make shipping containers.

There were only a few cars in the parking lot. Signs of a quiet day or a struggling business? Conor wondered.

"I think this must be some satellite office," Nicky said, as if reading his mind. "Vallencourt Logistiques is a large, international company. It deals with all manner of *logistiques*, not just trucking."

The company sign on the building had red lettering in a bold font with a steep angle to the right, as though the words were barreling forward against a headwind. Good imagery for a logistics company, Conor thought, and also symbolic of the direction his own instincts were taking since he'd first seen the diamond in Kate's hand.

During the ride, he'd had more time for reflection while Nicky and Reid talked in the front seat, and his thoughts were leaning in an unexpected direction. Despite apparent evidence to the contrary, a whispering intuition was telling him their assumptions were wrong, that they were not, in fact, chasing a jewel thief.

And if that was true, then who—or what—*were* they chasing?

Chapter Ten

NICKY PULLED the RCMP squad car around and parked on the shoulder of the road in front of the building. As they exited the car, Conor tried to imagine Jimmy emerging from his taxi a few hours earlier, shivering in his suede jacket. The visual he summoned looked like a frightened young man, not a wily criminal. It prompted further half-formed thoughts, layered and complicated, but what came out of his mouth was less artful.

"Jimmy isn't the answer. He's only an eejit."

Reid and Nicky stared at him, and Conor realized he'd interrupted a conversation they assumed he was part of, but that he hadn't heard at all.

"Sorry. Never mind, just away in me own head."

"So? Where else does the thinking happen? Tell us," Nicky said. "You have some theory."

"Nothing so grand as that."

Reid leaned against the hood of the car, hands in his pockets. "Do you think we've made a mistake somewhere? That we're on the wrong track?"

"No, it's not that, either. Not exactly. Look, I'm sorry. I've nothing, really. Let's go check this place out."

"Okay." Taking him at his word, Nicky pulled on her gloves

and started for the door, but Reid stayed where he was, giving him a long, thoughtful look. Conor shrugged.

"It's only a hunch that . . . I don't know. I feel like something bigger is going on here."

Reid pushed away from the car and patted him on the back. "Hunches can be important, Conor. Don't ignore them."

"Believe me, I don't. I can't afford to."

Inside, it became clear this particular satellite in the Vallencourt constellation was not designed with guests in mind. The building had no foyer or reception area to ease their passage. When Nicky opened the exterior door and they stepped through, they were at once in a low-ceilinged, wood-paneled office, standing in front of four Vallencourt staff members. They sat at battered steel-gray desks facing each other, and all of them stared in slack-jawed amazement at this abrupt arrival of visitors. An odor of grilled onions filled the space, along with something else that Conor assumed came from the St. Bernard dog lying in the middle of the floor. There was a wire-caged radiant heater in one corner, coils glowing red. For a few seconds its mosquito-like buzz was the only sound in the room. Nicky was first to recover.

"*Mon dieu*, that smells good," she announced, smiling at the source of the onions, a middle-aged woman with frosted hair, and a fork frozen halfway between the plate and her mouth. Nicky continued in a clatter of French. Conor and Reid nodded and smiled at the part that sounded like her introduction of them, and at last the spell was broken. The Vallencourt staff came to life, moving to find chairs and pushing the dog to one side to make room for them.

After a few more rapid exchanges, Conor caught on to the names and a few phrases. The frosted-hair woman was Vivienne. The rail-thin, balding man named Gilbert was her husband. There was another man, younger and with three times the muscles, wearing bib overalls and a watch cap. Mechanic. No name given. Finally, a young woman named Ci-Ci, maybe early twenties. Fashion plate. The jewelry, the perfect nails and makeup, the facial expression that could have been a sign tattooed on her forehead saying "this job is not a good fit."

Just when it seemed he and Reid would be mere spectators to Nicky's interview, she wheeled around in her chair to face them.

"Your turn, now. We have been discussing who you are and where from, but that's all."

"That's all?" Reid looked skeptical. "You've been talking for at least five minutes."

"Chitchat, you know? Introductions *à la mode Canadien*. Weather, good places to eat in Magog. I told them you are working on an important case in the US, and now I think they are happy to answer questions in English?" Nicky looked for confirmation from the four staff members. They assented in soft, uncertain voices and she gave them an encouraging smile. "Let's try it, anyway. Plain English, no fancy police lingo. I will translate if needed."

Conor gave Reid a nudge. "You're the one with a badge. Or two. Take it away." He then watched Marshal Briggs "take it away" like Columbo—shaggy-dog friendly, apologetic. He all but scratched his head and squinted.

"Folks, I'm sorry to be interrupting your day. We sure appreciate your time and won't take too much of it. The fact is, there is a gentleman we're trying to locate. We think he might have some important information to share with us. We believe he was in this area just a few hours ago, and we're wondering if you saw him, spoke to him. I understand a taxi from Newport, Vermont dropped him off right here in your parking lot, so, we wonder if maybe . . ."

Reid trailed off. As soon as the word "taxi" left his mouth, the atmosphere in the room had stiffened.

Chapter Eleven

IN THE ROOM'S sudden silence, Gilbert and Vivienne locked eyes. The mechanic shifted in his chair and looked oddly satisfied. Ci-Ci remained unchanged. Conor couldn't tell if she hadn't understood, or if boredom had pushed her into a fugue state.

"Is he in trouble?" Vivienne asked Reid, in English.

"Well, ma'am, I wouldn't say that." Reid's courtly Virginia drawl oozed reassurance. "We just want to talk. Am I right to think I'm speaking about someone you know? Maybe he works for Vallencourt?"

The mechanic made a guttural sound and spat out a line of French like it was a bad taste in his mouth.

Nicky translated the outburst in a mild tone: "'It's a fucking joke to say he fucking works at all.'"

Gilbert spoke for the first time. "His name is Jimmy Denarro. He is the chief executive's . . . *comment dit?*" He finished in French, and it was one that Conor recognized—*beau fils.*

"He's the CEO's son-in-law?"

"*C'est ça.*" Gilbert nodded.

"Does he drive trucks for Vallencourt?" Reid asked.

Again the mechanic could not suppress his contempt, and in translating, Nicky sounded like she was reciting a nursery rhyme.

"'He could not work a stick shift any more than he can work his own dick.'"

Conor kept his eyes trained on the wall, biting the side of his cheek.

Vivienne sighed. "The CEO is Tracy Vallencourt. Her youngest daughter, Lucie, is part of the company, but she is more interested in her artwork. She married Jimmy Denarro, who is from New York, I think. He came today in a taxi and we asked, but he didn't say why. He was—"

She said something in French to Nicky, who nodded and said, "Jumpy. Stressed out."

"He took one of the company vans and left," Vivienne concluded.

"Did he mention where he was going?" Reid asked, but she shrugged.

"Probably he was going home?" Gilbert suggested. "To the Charlevoix region. Vallencourt manages shipping at Pointe-au-Pic. It's a small port on the St. Lawrence, in La Malbaie. Lucie directs that office. She and Jimmy live near there, in a chalet the family owns. The marriage was only one year ago, and things are—"

"They are very young," Vivienne interrupted, scolding her husband with a sharp glance. They'd not been asked to comment on the marital affairs of the Vallencourt family.

"Would you give us their address please, Vivienne?" Nicky asked.

"*Bien sur*, Sergeant. It is just before you reach La Malbaie, along the Route du Fleuve."

While she was writing out the address, Conor gave the mechanic a conspiratorial smile. "Sounds like he's not your favorite member of the family."

Before Nicky could translate, the mechanic had responded in English. "He is lazy. He likes the money, but not the work, and . . ." He leaned forward, as if to give his words greater leverage. "He is an *idiot*."

❄

THE SNOW WAS FALLING in stinging windblown sheets when they returned to the car. With the defroster on high, they remained parked for a few minutes to plan their next move.

"An idiot," Nicky said, winking at Conor. "Sounds like your intuition is tuned correctly. Crystal clear signal."

He laughed. "It was hardly a stretch, considering his maneuvers so far. I guess the next stop on our tour is La Malbaie."

"How far is it?" Reid asked.

"It's a four-hour drive north . . . in good weather," Nicky said. They all looked past the flapping windshield wipers at the road, where the snow had entirely obscured its yellow line.

"The Crown Vic will be okay; it does fine in the snow." She glanced in the rearview mirror at Conor's sudden grimace. "It does, really. No kidding around."

"No, I believe you. I wasn't thinking about the weather."

Reid turned in his seat to face him. "New York. I haven't forgotten."

Confused, Nicky twisted to squint at both of them. "Forgotten what? What's in New York?"

"Ehm, there's a sort of party. An engagement party." Conor cleared his throat. "Mine, in fact. We're—Kate and I, my fiancée— we're flying to New York early tomorrow morning."

"Ah, okay, okay." Nicky looked amused by his lack of enthusiasm. She appeared ready to hear more, but he had no intention of getting into the details.

"It's a long story. Anyway, the point is . . ." He trailed off, searching for the right words to frame the predicament he found himself in, and felt guilty for resenting as much as he did. The prospect of scurrying home like a child out past his bedtime was embarrassing on its own, but it was more than that.

He had no dog in this fight; the diamond didn't belong to him or anyone he knew and he'd tagged along for a bit of a lark. A helpful distraction, as Kate had said. It shouldn't matter that much to him how it all turned out, but each discovery deepened his conviction of a larger picture than the one they were seeing. Leaving the challenge for others to pursue was maddening, but he saw no way around it. While he was fumbling to state the obvious, Reid came to his rescue.

"The point is, it's after two o'clock, the next clue is at least a four-hour drive north through a blizzard, and God knows how long it will take us to find it once we get there. Conor needs to head for Vermont while he still has a chance of making it home tonight, which means you're stuck with just me, Nicky. Now, I can have a squad car sent to Derby Line if we can get him—"

"Whoa, whoa. Reid. Wait. Stop." Nicky flashed the flat palm of her hand at the police chief, silencing him. "I can't be stuck with just you. Sorry. With just him?" She jabbed a thumb back at Conor. "That works, but not with just you. *Non.* It's not personal, okay? It's political. The request to Ottawa came from the UK, not the US. It came from British intelligence and it was exactly this: to render assistance to an operative in the field. That. Operative."

Nicky emphasized this with a few more jabs in his direction while Conor closed his eyes in resignation and tried to sink out of sight. Knowing what he would see, he opened them to face Reid's startled gaze.

"Who in the *hell* did you call?"

"I didn't know he'd play it like that. I only asked him to get us over the feckin' border. The whole 'Her Majesty's Secret Service' shite was not my idea. That is *not* what's going on here," Conor added, addressing Nicky.

"No kidding," she said, with a wide smile. "But it's better than a day of paperwork in Sherbrooke. So, since we are all stuck with each other, which direction are we going? North to La Malbaie, or back to the border?"

Reid stared out his side window, conspicuously quiet. At last, groaning, Conor scrubbed a hand over his face.

"Bloody hell. North to La Malbaie."

"Thought so." Nicky smirked, shifted the car into gear, and eased it onto the snow-covered road.

Reid's stiffened posture relaxed. "Thanks, Conor. I'll still do my best to get you home tonight."

"I know. Never mind about it. Can't be helped. It's not our fault this gom lives four hours away, and we can't control the weather. "

He was sure to be using all those lines again before long with Kate. Conor hoped they would sound more convincing the second time.

Chapter Twelve

OPENING A KITCHEN DRAWER, Abigail pulled out a cell phone and waved it at Kate. "You know he's not good with them. He left it right here on the counter this morning."

"Oh, for God's sake." Kate rolled her eyes. "I really don't understand what the phone thing is all about; it's not like he's a technophobe. He fixes my computer all the time."

"But you know nothing at all about computers," Abigail said.

"So?"

"I'm just saying it's a low bar."

"Anyway," Kate said, with exaggerated patience, "he could have borrowed one. The last I heard he was heading for the Canadian border, but that was hours ago. It's after four o'clock and I'm starting to— No, never mind." She made a scrubbing motion, physically erasing the thought. "I will *not* worry every time I don't know where he is."

"Why not?" Abigail dropped the phone back into the drawer. "He paces like a lost dog when he doesn't know where you are."

"Well, he's neurotic. I'm not and don't plan to be. We'll both just need to get used to not knowing where the other is sometimes." Kate sighed. "Anyway, I was the one who volunteered our help, so I can't complain. I should have known it would get complicated, especially once Frank got involved."

They both jumped at the sound of a hollow crash and stifled scream near the stove. One of the inn's staff members, Darla Barstow, had lost her grip on a hanging copper kettle. Refusing to acknowledge the racket, Abigail attempted an attitude of zen-like tolerance.

"Is it not working out?" Kate asked in a low voice. "We could put her back at the front desk."

"With a holiday party in the library and reservations for forty-eight in the dining room? It has to work out. I need every warm body I can get." Her chef arched an eyebrow. "Especially since the owners of the place are otherwise occupied."

"Sorry. Our timing for adventure isn't the best. I'm free now, though. Give me a job."

Kate spent the next hour shuttling drinks from the bar to the library and dirty dishes from the library to the kitchen, until, during one pass through the main hallway, she found three men standing at the registration desk. The two taller ones she pegged as FBI agents, although their identical black jackets didn't identify them as such. They were both middle-aged, well groomed, and sober faced. The third was a much older and shorter man, wearing a bright orange down jacket that looked as though pumped full of air. His suitcase looked half as tall as he was.

"There you are. I hope you haven't been waiting long." Hurrying forward, Kate put her tray of empty glasses on the desk and extended a hand. "I'm Kate Chatham. You must be Agents Knox and Toomey?"

"Yes, ma'am, I'm Pete Knox." The agent's handshake was brief and firm. "I'm afraid we're the ones who have kept you waiting. There was an accident on the interstate near Springfield."

The second agent offered an apologetic smile and a nod of greeting. Like his partner, he had dark, close-cropped hair, but with an added touch of silver at the temples. "Justin Toomey," he said, and then extended an arm, as if to sweep forward the smaller man next to him. "This is Dr. Aldo Gasparini, one of the country's finest gemologists and a consultant for the Bureau."

"It's an honor to meet you, Dr. Gasparini." Kate gave him a nervous smile. "I'm hoping the long trip will be worth your time. If this diamond turns out to be cubic zirconia I'll be mortified."

Stepping forward, the smaller man took her hands with exaggerated tenderness and gazed at her. "My dear Mrs. Chatham." His voice had a slight inflection that she assumed was Italian. "Your diamond could be made of paste and the trip would still be worth it. This charming inn, and the sight of you alone, makes it worth it."

"Well . . . thank you. Please call me Kate."

"A beautiful name. For a beautiful woman. And I beg that you will call me Aldo."

Startled, she glanced at the two agents. Their carefully bland faces only betrayed a hint of weary familiarity. She extricated herself from the man's grip by offering to take his coat. Once shorn of the ballooning orange jacket, he looked small, frail, and arthritic. The halo of white curls on his head made her think of lambswool. Kate's attitude toward him softened.

"Why don't we start with some dinner?" she suggested. "We're going to be packed tonight, but I can fit you in before the crowds descend."

She stored the suitcase behind the registration desk, and as she led them to the dining room, Agent Knox took a quick step forward to walk beside her. His stony expression had turned apologetic.

"I'm sorry about that. Aldo is harmless, but a little . . . eccentric. I couldn't say much when I called, with him sitting next to me in the car. He really is one of the best gem experts in the world, though."

"It sounds like he has an Italian accent?" Kate asked. "How long has he been in the country?"

The agent snorted. "Since birth. He's from East Boston." He smiled at her muffled laugh. "We've figured out that things go better if we humor him."

Kate made sure her dinner guests received prompt service, and when they'd finished Aldo insisted on paying his compliments to the chef. He delivered them with the passion of a man composing a sonnet while Abigail, flushed from the heat of the kitchen, stood staring at him.

Sensing her dangerous impatience, Kate steered the gemologist away and toward the office before Abigail could open her mouth. She rarely visited it since Dominic had taken on management duties the previous winter and was always amazed at how spotless he kept the desk. It took only a minute to sweep it bare for Aldo's "portable laboratory." Agent Toomey had wheeled the hard-shelled case inside the door, but they all agreed it made sense to have a look at the gem itself before unpacking anything.

Pulling as much drama as possible from the moment, Aldo examined his workstation from all angles while Kate and the agents watched. Apparently satisfied, he removed a square of black velvet from the pocket of his tweed jacket and, with a flourish, snapped it open and floated it to land at the center of the desk. He sat down, elbows braced against the surface, the tips of his fingers steepled together. He looked like a wizened child.

Reciprocating the slow nod he made in her direction, Kate moved to the safe, a participant in his solemn ritual. The atmosphere wavered a bit when she presented the treasure. She hadn't known whether or not was still needed, but had decided to keep everything as they'd found it, so Kate placed the Marlboro box on the square of velvet. Behind her, Agent Knox muffled a cough.

Dr. Gasparini looked at it for a period Kate thought longer than necessary, drumming the tips of his fingers together. Just when the last grains of her patience were slipping away, his hand darted out, snatched the box, and popped it open. Once the diamond was resting in his palm, his mood abruptly changed, becoming less theatrical, but more excited.

"My God. Bring the case," he said, his eyes fixed on the gem. "The case, please. Bring it. Bring it. Bring the case."

Chapter Thirteen

THE TWO AGENTS were in their element, familiar with the contents of Aldo's laboratory, but Kate found the action hard to follow. They rapidly unpacked a series of smaller cases and boxes, and from those emerged tools and instruments that looked better suited to a hospital lab. The only thing she recognized was a microscope, but several other items also had names ending in "scope." There were tiny brown bottles with unidentified liquids, a small lamp that gleamed a band of ultraviolet light, and something called a refractometer that at first appeared to be missing but turned up after another search laced with muttered obscenities.

Within a few minutes, the Biedermeier desk was unrecognizable, except that Aldo still sat behind it like a prince reviewing the gifts presented to him. He selected a small cylinder from the desktop and attached it to his eye, then gave them all a dismissive wave.

Agent Toomey leaned in and spoke next to Kate's ear. "He wants us out. Oddly enough, for this he doesn't like an audience."

Agent Knox made a tour of the windows, pulling down the shades to create a more dramatic pool of light from a work lamp on the desk. With this last step in the ceremony finished, they crept from the room, and Kate shut the door soundlessly behind them.

Relaxing at last, the three of them looked at each other and laughed.

"Good Lord, he's exhausting!" Kate said.

"Yeah," Agent Knox agreed. "If he wasn't worth it, we'd never put up with him. Is it okay if we wait in there?" He nodded across the hall toward the public living room, where flames were crackling in the large fireplace.

"Of course, but wouldn't you rather check in to your rooms?" Kate asked.

Toomey wrinkled his nose, rejecting the idea, and Knox agreed. "We should probably stay close, keep an eye on Aldo."

"You said he was harmless," she reminded him.

"Oh, he is, but he can get weird. We took him to a conference on Sanibel Island once and he showed up on the beach naked."

"Yup. Living room. Go on in," Kate said. "I'll bring coffee."

While waiting, Kate reported to Abigail for another assignment, wanting to be helpful but also needing distraction. She'd checked for any voicemail messages left on their private phone, and then at Dominic's station where the inn's main line rang during the evening hours. Still no word from Conor. Kate attempted an attitude of simple annoyance, but as she moved through the dining room clearing tables, worry sat at the corner of her mind like an itch needing to be scratched.

She expected a long wait for Aldo's report, but less than thirty minutes later, while delivering Caesar salads to a party of six, she heard a door thrown open and a high-pitched laugh in the front hallway.

"Oh, God." Kate smiled an apology at the six faces looking at her and quickly distributed the plates. "Table eleven needs grated cheese," she said, passing a waitstaff member as she bolted from the dining room.

When she reached the registration area, the FBI agents had already shuffled Aldo back into the office. Bracing herself, she opened the door and let out a gusty breath. The gemologist was circling the room. He could hardly contain his excitement, but he was fully clothed.

"I knew it, I knew it the minute I saw it. I had to make sure. Due diligence. Take the measurements—shape, proportions, weight. And it was 94.8!" Aldo threw up his arms in triumph. "I knew it would be. 94.8 carats, of course, and D-color. No doubt. No doubt about it."

Seeing Kate, he veered from his circular path and hurried toward her, but stumbled as he approached. She reached out to keep him from falling. He collapsed against her and clung there, knocking her back against the wall.

"Oh my dear woman. You take the cake," he said, still cackling. "Evalyn's father told her that, when she smuggled it home on her honeymoon. 'You take the cake.'"

The two agents had closed in and were roughly grabbing him. Although still dazed, Kate motioned them to stop.

"Evalyn who? What honeymoon?" She pushed him away but kept a gentle grip on his shoulders. "Let's just breathe a little, okay? Help me catch up. Are you saying you recognize the diamond, Aldo?"

"It's the star, my dear. It's the long-lost star, and you found it." He gave her a delighted grin, as his voice dropped to a whisper. "You found the Star of the East."

Chapter Fourteen

IT TOOK ALMOST AS LONG to settle down Aldo as he'd taken to identify the diamond. Kate persuaded him to sit on the office sofa and brought him a glass of his preferred nightcap—Madeira. It surprised her to discover they even stocked it. When he seemed calm enough to recount what he'd discovered, Kate sat down next to him, and the two agents pulled chairs over to face the sofa.

From his measurements and analysis, matched against the documentation available for the gem, Aldo expressed absolute confidence that they were looking at the Star of the East.

Mined from its likely source on India's Deccan Plateau in the nineteenth century, it had first appeared in the collection of the last Sultan of the Ottoman Empire, and had traveled the world several times before its astonishing recent appearance inside T-Dell Dunbar's deer.

"The Sultan got deposed in 1909." Extending a pinky, Aldo took a sip from his glass, but the continental accent had disappeared, replaced by one more in keeping with his Boston roots. "But even before that, the Star somehow got to Paris and into the hands of Pierre Cartier. He sold it to Evalyn Walsh McLean. Naturally, you've heard of her."

Agents Knox and Toomey reacted to the name, but Kate was

pretty certain she had never, in fact, heard of Evalyn Walsh McLean.

"She was a famous socialite in the 1920s and '30s," Agent Toomey explained. "The McLeans were like a royal family in the DC area. Evalyn and her husband, John McLean, are most famous for owning the Hope Diamond."

"Cartier again!" Aldo crowed. "He sold Evalyn the Star of the East on her honeymoon and she joked about smuggling it into the States on her ocean liner. A few years later they were back in Paris to buy the Hope. She wore them together on the same necklace." He leaned toward Kate. "She was wearing both when she died. Of course, the Hope became more famous."

"Who got the Star of the East after she died?" Kate asked him.

"Harry Winston bought it."

"Oh!" At last, a name Kate recognized.

Her brother once told her a story about the two of them meeting the famous jeweler as an elderly man, at her grandmother's apartment in New York. Kate had been three years old and couldn't remember it, but Peter swore Mr. Winston had pulled a 75-carat diamond from his pocket for them to look at.

"Harry bought the Hope Diamond, too. In fact, he bought Evalyn's entire collection," Aldo said, basking in Kate's undivided attention. "She had a tragic life. Her husband went into an insane asylum, a car ran over her son, her daughter died from sleeping pills—"

"Aldo." Agent Knox leaned forward, elbows on his knees. "Winston gave the Hope Diamond to the Smithsonian. Did the Star of the East go with it?"

"An excellent question." Intent on extending his moment with Kate, the diminutive gem expert drained his cordial glass and swiveled to her, closing one eye in a tipsy wink.

"Aldo," Agent Toomey snapped.

"No, no, no." Aldo sat up a little straighter. "Not the Smithsonian. Harry sold the Star of the East to the King of Egypt. King Farouk. Who never paid for it! Farouk got deposed too, kicked out in 1952. After a while, the Egyptians let Harry have his diamond back. He sold it to a private collector, and then bought it back again. A few years after he died, the Met hosted an anniversary reception for his company. Let me tell you, a lot of diamonds at that event, including the Hope and the Star of the East. That was over twenty years ago, and no one has seen it since."

"So, it wasn't really lost, then," Kate said, feeling this was an anticlimactic end to the story. "Harry Winston Jewelers has probably been keeping it in one of their vaults."

"Maybe." Aldo drew the word out, smiling. "Or maybe not. My colleagues and I have speculated about it for years. Stones with that kind of quality, value, and pedigree? They are the Hollywood celebrities of my profession! They're tracked, studied, evaluated. We know where they are and when they change hands. We talk about their public appearances, but we can't do that with the Star of the East, because it disappeared. Harry Winston, Incorporated always refused to say whether or not they had it, but if they did—"

"Why wouldn't they have reported it stolen?" Kate finished the thought for him.

"Why indeed? It's very odd, isn't it?" Still holding the cordial glass, Aldo pointed it like a baton at her and then at each of the FBI agents. "Very, very, very odd."

Chapter Fifteen

"YOU HAVE CONTROL ISSUES."

"Sorry?" Conor tore his attention from the road to look at Nicky's shadowed profile. After stopping in Quebec City for gas, Reid had insisted on giving him a turn in the front seat for the last leg of the journey, a courtesy he was appreciating less once twilight had given way to full darkness.

Nicky nodded at his hands—clenched—and his feet, where his boot was indeed pressed so hard against the floor that a stronger man might have punched a hole through it by now.

"You are trying to drive the car."

"I'm only trying to help," Conor protested. "Since it's dark, and we're in a blizzard, and every few miles I see a warning sign with a picture of a feckin' moose on it. Will you tell me Nicky, where in the hell are we, at all? I thought this place was a shipping port on the Saint Lawrence. We're after climbing into the mountains for two hours and no water in sight."

Nicky shrugged. "It is the way to get there. This autoroute traverses the edge of the Laurentian Mountains." The car shuddered through a windblown drift and she adjusted her grip on the steering wheel. Conor did the same with his own, phantom version.

"It's an autoroute, is it? Looks like a ski trail. Feels like a ski trail."

"It *will* be going downhill very soon."

"Splendid. Can't wait." Nicky's big laugh filled the car, which made him smile. "It's not you, it's me."

"I know, I know," she said. "Control issues. Doctors would say there was some situation in your childhood that made you feel helpless."

"Sure they wouldn't have to go that far back," Conor said, "and they'd find more than one." To prevent any more discussion along that line, he changed the subject. "Is there a lot of shipping traffic on this river?"

"Certainly," Nicky said. "From the Atlantic, ships come into the Saint Lawrence, and in Montreal they enter the Seaway. Through locks and canals, they can go all the way to Lake Ontario."

"Carrying what, for instance?"

She waved a hand. "Wind turbines, sugar, soybeans. Anything. The port at Pointe-au-Pic loads forest products, most of it newsprint. There are newspapers all over the world getting their paper from here. It is also a very beautiful area. You will see it better in the morning."

"Hmm." Conor's noncommittal response neither accepted nor challenged the idea of not being where he was meant to be when morning arrived. Turning his attention to Reid, who'd been making calls in the back seat, he gave the acrylic shield between them a light tap. "Any news?"

"Not much," Reid said. "The FBI contacted the Jewelers Security Alliance. They put out an alert to their members, same with the American Alliance of Museums. Got nothing. So far, nobody is missing a diamond."

"So, finders keepers?" Conor teased, thinking the last bloody thing he needed was more net worth to trouble his sleep.

"Don't get your hopes up. I think we might get some ideas once the gemologist gives us a report. My staff sergeant says Kate called a few hours ago with an update on that. The FBI touched base with her and they were expecting to be at the inn within the hour. She was wondering if anyone had heard from us." Reid held the phone through the partition's opening. "I need to call my wife and let her know where I am, but do you want to give Kate a call first?"

Conor considered the idea, chewing his lip. "No, you go ahead. I'll call her in a bit."

He'd only mentioned being late for dinner the last time he'd spoken with Kate. Calling with the news that he might not get home at all tonight wasn't a conversation he looked forward to starting. He tried to take comfort from the fact that he couldn't be blamed for the situation, and that surely there would be a flight from somewhere in Canada the following morning. Still, he regretted the wasted opportunity. If only Kate were with him, they'd have the perfect excuse for dodging an event neither wanted to attend.

Even without being a starred attraction, her father's holiday party was one she often said she dreaded. Each year, in obedience to some twisted code of loyalty, Kate and her siblings dutifully appeared, posing for a set piece display of family values that Douglas Chatham did not possess.

They'd escaped attendance the previous holiday season because of a last-minute group booking at the inn. Until the engagement party angle surfaced, Conor had hoped it was the sort of solid excuse they could call upon year after year.

The minute he met Kate's father, he'd twigged him as a boastful, pompous twat. After the antics they'd pulled to get the wedding moved he was starting to resent her siblings as well, and didn't expect that to change over a few glasses of holiday cheer.

Given the circumstances, he accepted the party as an obligation they couldn't dodge—at least, not intentionally. He couldn't help it that his Watsonian role had taken him more than six hours from home, and that every mile and fresh development were increasing the odds of not getting back in time.

A minute later, Conor was facing the prospect of never getting back at all. Beyond a swirling veil of snow, an enormous dark shape loomed on the road ahead. It looked like a boulder and appeared to be rapidly rolling toward them. His foot slammed against the floor of the car at the same instant Nicky's was hitting the brakes. Behind him, he heard an explosive grunt from Reid as he crashed against the partition and the Crown Victoria began its inevitable skid.

Nicky spun the wheel left and right, as though it were the plastic prop on a gaming console, but the car and boulder continued advancing on each other. At the last minute, the boulder shifted, and as they slid past it on the passenger's side Conor glimpsed a flash of antlers and a bearded, horselike face. After one complete revolution, the police car went halfway around again and stopped, facing back in the direction they'd come.

"Are you all right, Reid?" Nicky asked, not taking her gaze from what Conor now recognized as a moose. It moved at a jaunty trot across the highway, heading for the woods without a backward glance.

"Yeah. Yeah, I'm good."

She eased the car to the side of the road and they watched until the animal melted into snow and darkness. Reid, sounding dazed, muttered something unintelligible, and Nicky rested her forehead on the steering wheel. Conor pressed himself into the back of the seat, considering the irony of his second close encounter with wildlife within twenty-four hours.

"Not a bloody sign in sight," he said, breaking the silence at last. "Sure they never cross where they're meant to, do they?"

After a deep breath, he joined in the breathless hilarity that began filling the car.

ONCE THEY STARTED in the right direction again, the route soon started descending as Nicky had promised, but in the manner of a roller coaster, which she'd failed to mention. The inadequate moose warnings disappeared, replaced by terrain alerts that looked even more alarming. The signs showed the silhouette of a cartoonish car tipping over the top of a triangle and careening down the opposite side. Each had the grade of the approaching hill stenciled beneath, sometimes with an exclamation point for emphasis. As they crested each one Conor felt an irrational panic that they'd reached the edge of a cliff.

They coasted into a valley and almost immediately began climbing again, giving him time for only a fleeting glimpse at Baie Saint-Paul, a village filled with twinkling holiday lights and warmly lit homes. With snowflakes swirling around Victorian clapboard houses and clinging to surrounding trees, the coastal town looked like a folk art painting come to life. As they passed through it, he at last caught sight of the Saint Lawrence River, visible only as a wide, ink-black stain on the southern horizon.

About fifteen minutes later, after another spiraling drive up the side of a hill and around one final hairpin turn, Nicky turned off the main road onto a hillside driveway with a massive villa at the end. Shrouded in darkness, it faced a vista that was probably spectacular in daylight. At that moment, it could have been a blank wall.

Grateful to be alive and off the icy Canadian roads, Conor wasted no time exiting the Crown Victoria. He walked a few paces up the driveway, stretching to loosen his clenched muscles, but tensed again as he saw a stir of movement farther up the driveway. A dark figure appeared, peeling away from the shadowed corner of the house. A figure with a rifle attached to it.

A second later, Conor felt a slight tug at his jacket just before a bullet shattered the headlight behind him.

Chapter Sixteen

AT THE SOUND of the rifle shot, all three of them reacted in unison. Nicky and Reid had the squad car for protection, but Conor had walked too far down the driveway to get back in time. He took a running dive to his right, landing on his stomach behind a small toolshed. It was a poor excuse for cover with a shooter less than twenty yards away. He rose into a crouch, hands sweeping for anything that could work as a weapon—rock, stick, chunk of ice. Finding nothing but handfuls of powdery snow, he swore under his breath.

"The feckin' Walther would be handy now, wouldn't it, Chief Briggs? But, oh, right: 'We aren't going to need that kind of firepower.'"

Pinning himself against the wall, he squinted into the darkness. With a good line of sight back to the car, he could see Reid crouched by the right tire in back, and in front he could make out the peak of Nicky's fur-lined hat. She was kneeling behind the open door on the driver's side. Neither of them could see him or each other.

"Anyone hit?" Reid asked in a low voice.

"Fine here," Nicky said, sounding surprised, but not frightened.

"Okay here too," Conor said, before remembering the tug of the bullet brushing past him. He ran a hand over his ribs, making sure he was telling the truth, but then froze as a second shot exploded against the grill of the car and a voice rang out when the echo faded. Both came from the area where he'd seen the figure emerge. It confirmed their adversary had advanced no further, and that the shooter was a woman.

"That was a warning shot, but next time it won't be," she yelled. "Whoever you are, I give you ten seconds to get out of here."

The threat—spoken in heavily accented English—was menacing, but the voice sounded terrified. A dangerous combination. Conor inched forward to peek around the edge of the toolshed, then stopped and watched in alarm as Nicky stood up and propped an arm on top of the car door.

"*Lâ lâ*, girlie, you should have thought about where to point those warning shots before busting my headlight. I don't know who you expected, but you are shooting at the Royal Canadian Mounted Police, and you just vandalized federal property. We are not going anywhere."

To Conor's relief, the response was not a burst of gunfire but a question, posed in a quavering voice.

"How do I know you're the police?"

Nicky anticipated the challenge and was already reaching inside the car to snap on every light the Crown Vic possessed. Pattern lights on the hood, rear window, and front grille flooded the driveway in hues of electric red and blue. Added to that, the car's one remaining headlight winked like a lighthouse. It captured the woman in a stuttering brilliance and she shrank back into the shadows.

"Good enough? Or you want the siren, too?" Slamming the door, Nicky continued in French as she began striding forward. She spoke in a commanding voice, beginning with the repetition of something that to Conor sounded like *tabernacle*.

Without another word, the woman dropped the rifle and crumpled to the ground. Conor stepped away from the toolshed and waited for Reid, who was sliding his gun into its holster as he came forward. Looking at him, Conor knew they were sharing the same stunned realization. At no point had the RCMP officer drawn her weapon. She hadn't even popped the thumb loop on her own holster.

"We must be in Canada," Reid said.

"Yeah," Conor agreed. "Sure we'll get ourselves in trouble if we hang around very long."

"Do you know what *tabernak* means?"

"Is that what she said? Haven't a clue, but the way she kept spitting it out, I'll wager it's not polite."

As they approached the corner of the house, he saw a glint of brass in the snow and bent to pick up the spent casing of the bullet that had missed him by no more than a millimeter. Conor felt a prickle of cold sweat on the back of his neck as he registered the hollow diameter of the shell.

"Jaysus. The size of it. Is it meant to drop an elephant?"

"A bear, probably," Reid said. "They've got a lot more of them up here."

Nicky had a tight grip on the shooter and was wrestling her up to a standing position. She'd also taken possession of the rifle. She passed it to Reid and pulled a flashlight from her belt, shining it into the woman's face.

"Lucie Vallencourt?"

The woman nodded, squinting and lowering her head. She couldn't be more than twenty, Conor guessed, shorter than Nicky, but not by much. She had a fit, muscular appearance, and her hair stood up in a spiky pixie cut, dark blond shot through with streaks of pink.

"You speak English?" Nicky demanded. Another nod. "Then speak it please, so these two can understand. Do you always shoot at people who come to visit?"

"I thought you were somebody else," Lucie Vallencourt whispered. She raised her head and her eyes locked on Conor. "I thought you were here to kill me."

He took a steadying breath but realized he wasn't surprised. Somehow, he'd known it would end up like this.

Chapter Seventeen

FROM DAYLIGHT INTO DARKNESS, they'd tracked a hapless thief they now knew to be an American named Jimmy Denarro. It felt longer, but they'd needed only eight hours to follow the man's trail from a truck stop in Vermont, across an international border, right to his front door. Whatever satisfaction Conor might have taken from the achievement, Lucie Vallencourt punctured it with her next piece of unwelcome news.

"I don't know where he is," she said, responding to Nicky's terse demand for her husband's location.

"*Voyons donc.*" The RCMP officer gave her a sour look. "Maybe I will believe it after you've told us everything you do know. Let's go inside."

She began marching her toward the door with a grim-faced Reid following, but Conor caught his arm, his finger still tracing the outline of the spent shell he'd dropped into his coat pocket.

"Can I borrow your phone?"

It wasn't the best timing, but his sudden need to call Kate was so urgent it couldn't wait another minute. Reid handed the phone over with a nod, needing no explanation.

Conor went back to sit in the diminishing warmth of the Crown Victoria, which was still strobing the yard with flashing lights. Inside the car, he hit a few switches that plunged the driveway into darkness again, and then dialed the inn's main number. By now, Kate's mood had surely passed from irritation to anxiety. He realized, to his shame, that he'd been waiting for this transition, counting on her relief to soften the news that he wouldn't be home tonight, and that his odds of making it to the party at all were shrinking by the hour. It was the strategy of a coward. He should have called her hours ago.

Dominic picked up from his station in the dining room. He confirmed Kate had been checking regularly for messages, and before going to look for her he clicked his tongue and banged the receiver down on his podium to bolster the reproach. Once she was on the line, Conor heard the relief he'd expected and berated himself again for causing needless worry when she'd so often had valid reasons to fear for his safety.

"Thank God!" Kate said. "I did my level best not to wring my hands, but it's so late. Where are you?"

"Sweetheart, I'm sorry. I should have called earlier than this."

Conor's voice caught with unexpected emotion. The moose incident could be more easily turned to humor, but as he stared at the spot where Lucie Vallencourt had appeared, rifle in hand, he didn't feel like laughing. If her first shot had tracked a little more to the left, an enormous bullet would have torn through the center of his chest, and Kate would have been receiving a very different sort of call tonight. Sensing his mood, her bantering tone faltered.

"What's wrong? Are you okay?"

"I'm absolutely fine." He focused on her voice, pushing away the morbid thought that a matter of inches could have prevented him from ever hearing it again. "It's only that things are getting complicated. As they do, whenever you and I get mixed up in anything."

"Isn't that the truth. Where are you?"

"Near a town called La Malbaie. We're at the house of our diamond boy. Turns out he's an American named Jimmy Denarro. He married into a wealthy Quebec family that owns a freight forwarding company. He's not here, but we're about to question his wife, and . . ." Conor ended with a sigh. "To be honest, that's about all I've got so far."

"After eight hours? I'm sure you've got at least a little more than that." He could hear Kate's patient amusement. "You sound travel weary, though, and I have news, so do you want me to go first?"

"Yes, please," Conor said.

He settled in to listen, but interrupted before she'd gone very far. "Hang on a minute. The FBI's diamond expert is *flirting* with you?"

"I'm not sure 'flirting' is the right word."

"But, that's what you just called it."

"Conor, Aldo is about eighty years old."

"Is he? Aldo. Cheeky old bollocks. Carry on, so."

Kate's story fascinated him. He'd begun to think of the diamond in an affectionate sort of way, as if it were a lost puppy they'd found wandering the road. It astonished him to hear the gem had once been connected with the Hope Diamond, and in the most literal sense—worn together on the same necklace. Now, one was an object of awe for museum visitors, while the other faded into obscurity, knocking about among owners until someone couldn't even be bothered to keep track of it.

"It must be worth millions," Kate said.

"No doubt," Conor said. "How can no one be missing the bloody thing? Between the value and its history, it's like some famous person disappearing without a trace."

"That's just how Aldo described it, as if a celebrity everyone had given up for dead suddenly showed up again."

"So, what's next? An FBI visit to Harry Winston's shop, I imagine?"

"Correct. I'll call and schedule a meeting with them in the morning."

"Will you, so?" He smiled, recognizing an entirely predictable scenario. "You've joined the FBI, have you?"

"I'm going to New York tomorrow, anyway. With you, as you recall. When do you think you'll get back?"

"Ehm, about that . . ." Conor paused, tried to start again, and failed. The silence at the other end of the line felt like it might go on forever, with only the faint background noise of a packed dining room telling him she was still there. At last, Kate cleared her throat.

"Where is La Malbaie, precisely?"

Drained of its usual warmth and color, her voice sounded toneless, and his heart sank. Wiping some condensation from the car's side window, he peered out, but the amorphous horizon showed no distinction between water and sky.

"On the St. Lawrence Seaway. I've no map to place it, but we drove at least two hours past Quebec City, so I'd say it's a fair whack."

"Why are you there?"

"Because we think this guy Jimmy might be—"

"No, I get that." Kate sounded more acerbic now. "I'm asking why *you* are there. Today was supposed to be a distraction, not a get-out-of-jail-free card. You couldn't let Reid go on without you?"

"As it turns out, I could not." Conor sighed. "It's because of Frank. He turned it all into some sort of interagency-cooperation bollocks, so apparently if I'm not involved, nobody is."

"Of course. The indispensable man."

"Kate, please—" He stopped. His plea lacked any conviction or force. He expected a hammer-and-tongs attack and knew he deserved every blow, for acting like a whining child about the party in the first place, and now for the prospect of causing humiliation for the most important person in his life by not showing up for it. He braced himself for the onslaught. When it didn't come, Conor realized he'd again underestimated her. Kate had training of her own to draw on, and, gathering herself, she did exactly that.

"Okay, we'll deal with it later."

He leaned back against the headrest. "Thank you."

"I'm not being kind. It's just that showing up alone at my own engagement party is not something I'm willing to contemplate right now. Anyway, I've given you my news so it's your turn. Let's have your report."

He filled in the details of their journey for Kate, but decided the recent gunplay was an item best left until he got home. While they talked, he kept an eye on the villa. On the first floor, most of the lights were on now, illuminating a handsome interior of polished wood and art-lined walls. He wondered what was going on inside, and a minute later Kate read his mind.

"You should get in there and see what's happening. Keep me posted?"

"I will, of course. Kate, I'm so sorry. I'll do whatever I can to be there in time." Conor appreciated the irony that the last party on earth he'd wanted to attend was now one he couldn't bear to miss.

"You'd better," Kate said, then relented with a short laugh. "Really, I'm just bitter to not be hundreds of miles away in another country myself. I suppose I'll cope the way I always have for Daddy's gruesome holiday parties. With martinis. The bartenders at the Pierre see me coming now."

He smiled. "Everyone sees you coming, Kate. Except when they don't."

Chapter Eighteen

FOLLOWING a snow-drifted path lined with evergreens, Conor made his way to a small covered porch and the villa's rear entrance. Before stepping into a ceramic-tiled entryway, he knocked a slurry of road sand and snow from his boots and swept a glance over the living room beyond it. It featured an abundance of pine wood, every visible surface polished and freckled with dark-stained knots. The wide-planked floors, the windowsills and door lintels, the caramel-shaded beadboard lining the walls—all of it so fresh and new he could detect the resin scent of it hanging in the air.

A stunning mantelpiece and raised hearth constructed of river rocks took up most of one wall in the living room, and from there the main floor's open plan flowed from living room to kitchen to a cozy den where a short but bushy Christmas tree stood in one corner, decorated with white lights and crimson ornaments. A common wall of windows ran the length of the space, looking out onto a deck with a view over the hillside to the St. Lawrence in the distance.

Conor found everyone in the kitchen area, and discovered he hadn't missed much. Lucie Vallencourt had been close to the edge of something before they'd ever arrived. Confronted with the profane anger of the Royal Canadian Mounted Police, coupled with the fact that she'd nearly shot a man, the young woman had reached her tipping point. Like the animated cars on the highway signs he'd seen, she had pitched over the top and down the side of steeply graded terrain. Sprawled at the table, head on her arms, she was convulsed in sobs.

"We are off to a slow start," Nicky admitted, as Conor sat down next to her.

The officer's blue anorak rested on the back of the chair she'd planted herself in, which was positioned to block Lucie from leaving her own. She'd also removed her hat, revealing a neatly wound bun of silvered brown hair. The hat itself, dripping snowmelt, lay in the middle of the table like a centerpiece. Its beaver fur glistened in the beam of the overhead light. Reid was on his feet opening and closing cupboard doors—of which there were many—searching for anything that might coax their subject into a state fit for questioning.

"There," Nicky called out as he hit upon a liquor cabinet. "Crown Royal. Bring that."

"I don't drink whiskey!" Without lifting her head, Lucie wailed as if the bottle were being poured down her throat.

"Okay, no whiskey," Reid soothed, his voice dripping honey. "How about a good old-fashioned cup of tea?"

She hiccuped, snuffled, and at last croaked something that sounded like acceptance. Nicky shared a glance with Conor. "Bring the Crown Royal, anyway, and at least two glasses. With a lot of ice."

Thinking the young woman's histrionics a bit overplayed, Conor rose from the table to stand at the large picture window it faced. Outside, the storm had finally relaxed, whittling itself to a lazy sputter of the larger flakes that always came last. The snow-covered deck had a railing on three sides, garlanded with evergreen and wound with the same white lights as the Christmas tree. Beyond its bright, twinkling border, the darkness was impenetrable.

He studied two framed canvases that hung on the wall flanking the window. They were landscapes. A set of gallery lights in the ceiling shone on each individual work. One was a wooded setting in early spring with delicate green shoots spiking through patches of snow. The other displayed a summertime scene—wildflowers banked on either side of a forest brook that shimmered where sunlight threaded a tangle of branches to touch it.

"These are beautiful," Conor said. "They're watercolors aren't they?"

He knew they weren't. At one time, he could not have named the materials used in a piece of art to save his life, but falling in love with a visual artist had expanded his education on many levels. The landscapes were pastels. Since he understood something about the effort required to master the technique, and since the signed canvases told him the artist was sitting with her face on the table behind him, Conor hoped his display of ignorance would get a reaction. He wasn't disappointed.

"What?" Lucie lifted her head. "Watercolors? No. These are pastels. Both of them."

"Are they, so?" Conor turned to face her, feigning uncertainty. "That's like chalk drawing, is it?"

"Of course it is not like chalk drawing," she snapped. "It is like pastels." She sat up straight, wiping the tears and smeared mascara from her face. With her pink-tipped hair standing on end, she reminded him of nothing so much as a stalk of bee balm.

"Oh." He shrugged and smiled. "Sorry. I haven't a clue about art, really. You're the artist?"

"I, ah . . . yes." Lucie focused on the steaming mug Reid placed in front of her. The transition from writhing hysterics to polite conversation seemed to confuse her.

"Well, these are lovely, anyway. They all are." Sitting next to her, Conor gestured at the paintings lining the walls of the den.

"Thank you." She took a cautious sip of tea, darting a look at him that quickly skittered away. "I'm sorry."

"That you almost shot a twelve-inch hole through the middle of me? Thanks. At the very least I'd say you owe me a few answers. Think you can help us with that, now?"

Lucie nodded, while a few tears made fresh tracks through what remained of her makeup.

Conor signaled he would yield the floor to either Reid or Nicky, but neither showed any desire to take it. Reid splashed a hint of whiskey into three ice-brimmed glasses and handed them around. He raised his own in salute and leaned back against the kitchen island. Settling in her chair, Nicky merely smiled at Conor, rattling her ice cubes with a finger.

"Fine." He drained the miserly ration of whiskey and turned to Lucie. "You told us you thought someone was coming to kill you. Who?"

"Mounir," she whispered. "Jimmy said he would probably come here."

Who the hell is he? Conor wondered, but didn't ask. He decided it was too early to admit how little they knew or understood and stuck with the primary goal that had brought them here. "When was the last time you saw your husband? Was he here at all today?"

"No, I haven't seen Jimmy since yesterday."

He sat forward, watching her. "You saw him *yesterday?* Where?"

"I'm trying to remember." She frowned. "It was some little town off the highway in Vermont."

He didn't offer the answer right away. Conor let her continue reaching for it while enjoying a telepathic eureka moment with his companions. Jimmy Denarro might still be missing, but they'd found the "person of interest" who'd been with him at the P&H truck stop. It was his own wife.

Chapter Nineteen

WELLS RIVER.

When Conor at last offered it, the name prompted an obvious twitch of recognition in Lucie. At the same moment, she appeared to realize she might have talked too much. Instead of responding to him, she took a half-hearted stab at changing the subject.

"Maybe it would be good to give you all a glass of wine."

As a stalling tactic it was hopeless, but Reid's revved-up Southern charm gave it the sheen of a gracious invitation.

"Well, that's real kind of you, but we should wait until you're finished."

"What is there to finish?" she asked, nervous and sullen. "You know everything about it, *non?*"

"We're missing a few details, which is why we're here," Conor said, impatient for the rest of the story. "Go on, now."

"Maybe I shouldn't. Maybe I need a lawyer?"

"I don't know," he shot back. "Do you?"

Lucie met the remark with a flash of anger. "No. I've done nothing wrong, but I need details, too. Who are *you,* anyway?" She pointed at Conor and then turned to fire several questions in French at Nicky, who responded in English with equal vehemence.

"Never mind who he is, or what we already know. If you

answer questions instead of asking them we will be finished sooner, and we will be grateful for your *cooperation*." Nicky put a heavy emphasis on the word and Lucie appeared to get the message.

"Yes, okay. So, tell me what details you are missing."

"Who was Jimmy meeting in Wells River?" Conor asked.

"Meeting? No one."

"But you left him there," he said, stating the obvious.

She looked embarrassed but then exploded again. "It was craziness, this business. Who knows what it is all about? It was one thing and then became another thing. A bad thing. Jimmy should not have involved my family's company. He should have refused to do it."

"To steal it, you mean," Conor said. "He should have refused to steal the diamond, but he didn't?"

"Steal?!" Lucie stared at him. "He stole nothing! We don't even know where it came from. It was in the container we got from the man in New York."

"The man in New York," he repeated, encouraging her to continue.

"Yes, Cyril."

"Cyril." Conor sighed at the mention of a second inscrutable name. "*Jaysus*. Okay. Will you ever just start over from the beginning."

"I thought you knew all these things." Exasperated, Lucie hiked her chin at Reid and Nicky. "RCMP, and he is New York police, *non*?"

The Hartsboro chief looked amused by the mistaken identity but his smile was brief. "I'm not from New York," he said. "Conor's right. Let's back up and start this story from the top."

Lucie clutched at her hair and released it with a hiss, as if its radiant pink tips had burned her fingers. She slumped against her chair. "Do you even know about my family's business?"

"We do, yeah. Vallencourt Logistiques. Go on." Conor thought the news of their visit with the Magog staff could wait.

"Our office here is at the port, Pointe-au-Pic," she said. "It's not so busy, maybe a few ships each week. Some of them dock here three, four times a year and we get to know the crews. Vallencourt performs some services. It is called . . . *Esti*, I can't remember." Lucie turned to snap at Nicky. "*On fait l'arrimage.*"

In French, they launched into an exchange so rapid that Conor could more easily assign a melody than any meaning to the words. Reid joined them at the table, heaving a pointed sigh as he took the chair next to Nicky. She gave a brisk nod and broke off in midsentence.

"Stevedoring," Nicky said. "Vallencourt handles the cargo operations at Pointe-au-Pic. Loading and unloading rolls of newsprint for container ships."

"Yes. Stevedoring," Lucie agreed, still looking fierce. "On Monday, the Hollumborg was in port for the night. Usually, the ships don't stay that long, but when they do, the crews will come into La Malbaie for the bars and Jimmy will always go with them. You see, he is—" She squinted, as if wondering how to explain something complicated, but quickly gave up. "He is just bored. All the time bored. And not satisfied. It's far from the cities, here. There's nothing to do. He doesn't like the work. My mother pays us a salary, he thinks it's not enough. He hates how quiet our life is." She gave an indifferent shrug dismissing it all. "It's too bad. I like a quiet life, and I don't need much money."

Bloody hell. Match made in heaven, Conor thought, as Lucie hurried on with her story. Jimmy had returned home early Monday night, excited. The Hollumborg had taken a container on board in Toronto by mistake. It was going to the Port of New York and that wasn't on the Hollumborg's route. It was going down the seaway, then stopping here again before going on to Alexandria. The captain—this was the "Mounir" she'd mentioned—wanted to pay Jimmy ten thousand dollars to freight-forward the container by truck to New York.

"Mounir said the company would cover expenses for us to stay two nights in New York City." Lucie rolled her eyes. "So we could have some fun."

She paused, and then grew defensive. "I didn't want to do it. I thought it was a bad idea. Why would they pay so much, I wondered. To be so worried about one container didn't make sense, but Jimmy had already told the captain we would do it."

"And the full name of this captain?" Nicky asked. She'd removed a leather-covered notepad from the pocket of her anorak.

"He's only called Mounir. I don't know his other name."

Nicky wrote it down with a few decisive strokes. "Physical description?"

"Oh, I don't know. Tall, very dark hair and eyes, thick eyebrows. He could be anyone from anywhere. A bit like this one. Handsome." She waved a hand at Conor, in a manner that told them all her intent was purely forensic.

Nicky grinned at him before resuming her attack on the notepad. "So, you agreed to the trip."

"I had to," Lucie said. "He arranged it all before telling me. The crane had already moved the container to one of our trucks. What could I do?"

"I suppose you could have told Jimmy to go without you," Reid suggested, then looked startled by her derisive laugh.

"He has no license for the truck. When it's needed, I do the driving." She sighed. "I was tired and didn't want a fight, so yes, I agreed, and it was all okay at first. The container was in order, the paperwork from the Hollumborg was correct. We left Tuesday morning and got to New York in the evening, and it was all as Mounir said. We drove to Red Hook Terminal and there was a man to meet us. That was Cyril. He said we could leave the truck at the terminal and come back for it Thursday. He gave the ten thousand dollars to Jimmy, told us everything was paid for at the Ritz Carlton and to go have a good time."

She glanced at Nicky. "He was not tall or short, or handsome. He was bald, with a gray beard."

"And did he look like he could be from anywhere?" Reid asked.

"He is Egyptian. A Coptic Christian from Alexandria. He came to New York with his family six years ago."

Although peculiarly specific, Lucie offered the details as if they were incidental.

"Some fairly personal information there," Conor remarked. "Cyril just burbled all that out for you, did he?"

"No, it was because—" She snapped her fingers at Nicky's notepad. "May I?"

Nicky pushed it across the table along with her pen and they watched as Lucie sketched. It was a symbol, and to Conor it looked like one he knew, but rendered differently. In its Celtic form, the Christian cross featured a circle centered over the spot where its lines intersected. In Lucie's drawing, the circle was not around the intersection but sitting above it, with its own smaller cross inside it. She completed the sketch by adding a looping line to indicate a necklace.

"He was wearing this." She turned the pad to give them a better angle. "It was real gold, I think. Quite beautiful. I asked about it and he told me it is a Coptic cross, done in the old style."

They studied the drawing in silence, until Nicky reclaimed her notepad. She flipped to a fresh page, but for a few more seconds Conor's attention remained fixed, as if the image were still there. It might not mean anything, but the sketch had started the back of his neck tingling. He'd seen the same symbol the night before, traced on the front of the Marlboro box.

Chapter Twenty

LUCIE DISMISSED the two nights in New York with an air of boredom, as though one of the most exciting cities in the world wasn't a patch on the delights of La Malbaie.

The couple returned to Red Hook Terminal at noon on Thursday. Cyril was there again to meet them, and he had a surprise. He had placed another container on the Vallencourt truck, which the Hollumborg would pick up Friday evening, when it stopped at Pointe-au-Pic before heading on for Alexandria. Its only cargo was a box of New York Yankees souvenirs for the crew. Lucie and Jimmy could leave the truck at the pier and the crew would use the ship's crane to lift the container on board.

"He thought we were both fools." Lucie made a sour face. "Once we'd left, the fighting started. Cyril gave us paperwork, but he had already locked the container, so we never saw the cargo and he gave us no key. This wasn't correct. Jimmy said it didn't matter, that everyone at Derby Line knows Vallencourt and wouldn't stop us."

"Is that true?" Conor directed the question to Nicky and she nodded.

"Cyril and Mounir knew what they were doing. As long as the

paperwork was in order, the border patrol would wave them through. Vallencourt has a spotless reputation."

"Yes." Lucie jumped on this observation. "It insulted my family. We don't allow cargo we haven't inspected. We don't transport containers we can't unlock!"

Ending with a shout, she lurched up to grab a bottle of Bordeaux from the solid oak buffet behind her. Opening one of its shallow drawers, she snatched out a corkscrew and thrust it at Conor, along with the bottle.

"Whether you want any or not, open it. I'm having some wine."

"Happy to. Just keep talking while you drink," he said, but thought he could guess where it was all heading. "The truck's container didn't stay locked, obviously."

"No." She moved to a cupboard and, after an inquiring look at all of them, returned with a single wineglass. He slid the opened bottle forward and she poured generously. "We fought all the way through New York and Vermont, and at this Wells River place I broke the lock. I wanted to check that it wasn't drugs or guns, you know? So, fine. Baseballs, gloves, and team shirts, like Cyril said. Then, when we were putting it all in the box again, I saw something all the way at the back. At first, it looked like someone had dropped a cigarette box, but it was taped to the wall. When I ripped it off the top came open and . . . there was a diamond. A huge diamond. Imagine seeing that fall out of a stupid cigarette box."

Conor could well imagine it, having experienced it himself.

Lucie took a large swallow of wine, and suddenly looked exhausted. "We should have called the police, but we were too afraid. Jimmy put it in his pocket and said he would carry it until we'd crossed the border, but I couldn't do it. Not in a Vallencourt truck. I told him we needed to travel separately. He should take a taxi from Newport and we would meet in Magog, but he wouldn't agree. So, when he went into the men's room . . . I drove away."

Cheeks coloring with emotion, she looked defiant, as if daring them to scold her, but Conor had no intention of it. All things considered, it was a bloody clever trick and he rather admired her chutzpah.

"Is that the last time you spoke with him?" he asked.

"No. He called my mobile phone right away." For the first time, she offered a faint smile. "He was almost too angry to speak. I said I would wait for him in Magog, but he said not to bother, so I came home. He didn't call again until late last night, and it was very short. He was in Newport and said everything had gone wrong and our lives might be in danger but he would try to fix it. That was all. I don't know where he is, or where that diamond is, either."

"Neither does Jimmy," Nicky remarked, still focused on filling up her notepad.

Lucie froze while reaching for the wineglass. "You found him? Why didn't you tell me this earlier?"

"Not him. We found the diamond," Reid explained. "We connected a few dots and tracked him to Magog. He did end up at the Vallencourt office there, but where he went next is a mystery. Thought we'd find him here."

"But the diamond?" Lucie asked, urgently. "You have it with you?"

Reid cleared his throat and colored slightly. "Uhh. No, we don't. It's in Hartsboro Bend, Vermont. That's where it was found after Jimmy lost it."

"Lost it? He *lost* it?!" They watched her confusion shift to an incandescent rage. "*Quel imbecile!* No wonder he thinks they will kill us! *Là, là, mon dieu.* Why did this fool come back at all?"

She reached again for the wine bottle, but Conor swept it out of reach, his patience at an end. He shared Reid's chagrin that they didn't have the diamond with them. It might have been a useful bargaining chip for whatever was coming, but they couldn't have known the escapade would lead them to this point, and they had no notion of the direction it was going next. What he did know was that his nerves were fired with danger signals, and the time for coddling the "person of interest" was over.

"The 'fool' didn't come back for his own safety." Conor secured the cork with a heavy bump of his fist. "Has it occurred to you at all that he was worried for yours? No, none of that." He raised a finger as her eyes began filling again. "Hold yourself together, because we haven't got all night, have we? What time did the Hollumborg arrive at the port?"

The icy tone of command worked. Lucie wiped her cheeks and swiveled to an elaborately carved cuckoo clock on the wall.

"I don't think it has," she said softly. "It is scheduled for nine o'clock."

"And where's the truck?"

"I left it at the pier last night, as Cyril told us. I couldn't think what else to do."

"Brilliant," Conor said, glancing again at the clock. "So, the ship arrives in less than two hours, and not long after the crew is going to be lifting aboard a container with a broken lock. That will interest someone enough to have a peek inside, and once they discover their crate full of baseball gear is missing a souvenir, they'll be looking for the truck drivers. I imagine plenty of people in the bars downtown know where you live, and I'm guessing you've run all this through your head a few times already, which is why you met us in the driveway with a bloody great rifle. You thought they'd arrived early, I suppose?"

Without waiting for her reply, he turned to Reid and Nicky. "We need a plan."

Chapter Twenty-One

NICKY APPEARED startled by his clipped delivery, but Reid's response was swift. "My thoughts exactly, and fast. First step is to get the witness to safety. Lucie, you'd better go pack an overnight bag so we can move you out of here. Just one. The basics."

Conor maintained a neutral expression, hiding his surprise. Over the past few minutes, he'd been speeding along a single track and was taken aback to realize the police chief wasn't with him on it. Thinking it wise to show a unified front, and knowing he could make good use of the time once she was out of the room, he gave Lucie a nod of encouragement. As she sped away and upstairs, Nicky tucked the notepad back into her pocket, regarding them thoughtfully.

"You're sure someone will come tonight?"

"They'll have to," Conor said. "Because they're likely even more terrified than Jimmy and Lucie. Cyril from the Port of New York didn't steal that diamond, and I don't believe it's meant for Captain Mounir or anyone else on that ship. They're all just playing their part, chauffeuring the thing out of the country and across the ocean for someone else. We've no idea who, but I think it's safe to say this is no ordinary jewel heist."

"Why is that?" Nicky asked.

"Well, for one thing," Reid said, "there's been a nationwide alert out for over twelve hours and we still don't have anyone reporting it stolen, which is damned strange. Either they don't realize it's gone, or don't want to admit it."

"Which might be because it's no ordinary jewel," Conor added. "I haven't filled you in on the latest. When I talked to Kate, she said the FBI's gemologist had showed up at the inn, and he identified the thing within twenty minutes. It's got a pedigree as long as your arm and has been missing for years. He's dancing 'round the place like he found Amelia Earhart having a pint at Heathrow."

After a rapid account of the history and significance of the Star of the East, Conor took a breath and faced Reid. He expected a difficult conversation, and tried to begin it gently.

"I understand your instincts, but we can't take her out of here. You must realize that? Whatever is going to happen, she needs to have a role in it."

"No." There was a sharp finality in Reid's reply. "One or two of us can stay, but it's too dangerous to have a witness on the scene."

"Lucie's not a witness, Reid. She's a participant. It makes no sense for us to be here if she's not. What kind of charge could Nicky bring? We've a diamond that turned up in a deer carcass on a back road in Vermont. No one's missed it so far, and whoever it was meant for isn't going to get it. Also, we've a story that's too crazy not to be true but not a shred of hard evidence that it is. It all adds up to zed, and if this Mounir fellow turns up, he'll know it. We'll get nothing out of this tonight if we don't—"

"No. No."

Agitated now, Reid snapped the glasses from his face and began rubbing the lenses with a napkin. Thinking she must agree with him, Conor turned to Nicky in silent appeal. Looking uncomfortable, she picked up her hat and hopped from her chair as though it had burst into flames.

"I saw a side road behind some trees, running parallel to this house. I'm going to move the Crown Vic over there in case someone shows up before we're finished ... discussing this plan." She pulled the hat on but then paused, laying a hand on Reid's shoulder. "For what it's worth, he's right. I can't arrest a man just for knocking and asking a couple of strangers if they've seen his friends."

As soon as the door closed behind her, Conor slid to sit across from the man he'd known for only a day but already liked better than many he'd known for years.

"This is what you asked for, isn't it?" He smiled. "A wingman with experience."

Reid gave a shaky laugh, his head still bent over his glasses. "Looks like I got more than I bargained for."

"Mmm, I've heard that before; but sure look." Conor leaned forward. "You've shedloads more than I have, and you know I'm right. So, what's the story?"

"The story." Reid winced at the term. "The story is simple. I'd just rather not repeat past mistakes."

Past mistakes. Of course. Conor felt a rush of insight, mixed with a healthy dose of empathy. "I think what you're saying is you'd rather not repeat whatever fiasco ended up with you as a town cop in the back-arse of nowhere. Is that about it?"

Reid put his glasses back on, adjusting the fit, then looked up with the truth in his eyes. Conor nodded.

"I know how it feels, mate. I promise you that. Someday we'll swap chapter and verse, but at the minute it's the one thing we can't think about or we'll end up with new mistakes on top of the old. Now, as I said earlier, I don't think Mounir is the main target, but he's caught up in this scheme and he knows something. If we're going to catch the bastard tonight, we need to force his hand, and the only way I can think to do it is to let him come for Lucie. If he believes she's in here alone, he'll be even more likely to act."

Reid sighed. "You think it's worth the danger we'd be putting her in?"

Conor grimaced. "Listen, I don't much like it, either, but I think we can all see there's something fairly serious going on here, and I can't think of another way to get the result we need. Tell me if there's a better option and I'm not coming up with it."

"There isn't a better one. You're right. You and Nicky, both." Reid poured them a bracer from the bottle of Crown Royal.

"Do you want me to tell Lucie?" Conor asked.

"No, I'll do it. Wingman." He raised his glass. With relief, Conor watched the creased face relax back into good humor. "In the original military sense of the term, of course."

Conor laughed. "Jaysus, I should hope so."

Chapter Twenty-Two

ALTHOUGH GENTLE IN HIS PERSUASION, once Reid began describing the situation to Lucie, he came straight to the point. Until they had some cause for arresting Mounir, the only people with a proven connection to the diamond were Jimmy, and her. The message wasn't subtle, but it proved unnecessary.

For the first time, Lucie seemed to understand what fear and a volatile temper had prevented her from seeing earlier—that the three of them were not enemies but allies who could get her out of the mess she'd landed in, and she had better help them do it. Conor welcomed the shift in attitude, and admired her bravery in rising to the challenge. Before Reid had even finished his pitch, she was already on board and surprising them with a valuable contribution.

"I found out where the Hollumborg is," she announced. "When I checked the marine traffic website a few hours ago the ship was still west of Quebec, but just now upstairs I looked again. It's approaching Isle-aux-Courdres."

"Does that mean it's on time?" Reid asked.

"Yes, and there are procedures for docking properly at Pointe-au-Pic, so it will be at least nine thirty before anyone can leave the ship or load cargo."

With this timeline to work with, they quickly patched together a plan, each adding something to the details, developing contingencies, identifying problems and solving them, all in the interest of avoiding a "fiasco."

The first objective was to seize the initiative with a reconnaissance of the port—to observe the transfer of the container after the ship's arrival and hopefully witness the crew's reaction. Pointe-au-Pic was a fifteen-minute drive away, and as the only one trained for the task who was also in civilian clothes, the job fell to Conor. He didn't love the idea of setting out again without "firepower," but he could hardly suggest he had more need of a gun than the two police officers, and the rifle seemed a bit much. As he prepared to leave in Lucie's SUV, armed only with her mobile phone, a thought occurred to him.

"When the crews come in to town, what's their favorite bar? Is there one Mounir might head to, looking for Jimmy?"

"La Grillade," Lucie said at once. "There are places around the port they like in summer, but in winter it's always La Grillade. That's where they went on Monday night."

Quickly, she sketched a map, marking the locations of both the port and restaurant. It was a ten-minute drive to the port, and the restaurant was just a few streets away from it.

"The place is easy to find," she said. "It looks like a type of Wild West building. The second floor is where they go. There is a bar and music on weekends."

Conor pocketed the map and grinned. "'Pioneers and alcoholics.' The *craic* will be mighty. I'll be back sometime tomorrow."

Lucie's cream-colored Chevy Yukon was the latest model, fully loaded and already trashed. The interior air freshener gave off a sickening tropical scent and the floor mats were invisible under a layer of dirt. The middle console held an arrangement of paper cups and shopping receipts that might have been an intentional piece of sculpture. It felt as big as a Winnebago. It drove like one, as well.

Easing the SUV down the steep driveway and onto the even more precipitously angled road, Conor noticed a plow had made at least one pass since they'd arrived. The temperature had dropped below zero, but the snow had stopped and the night sky was clear enough for a waxing moon to throw off a surprising amount of light. The Route du Fleuve continued its pattern of dips and loops on its way to the center of La Malbaie, but it was remarkably less hair-raising now that he was in control of the vehicle and could actually see something. Really, the road was nothing compared to some of the more spine-chilling lanes winding through the cliffs of the Dingle peninsula.

He followed a steep descent through landscapes with homes scattered among fields glowing blue-white under the moonlight. The houses grew more thickly clustered as he approached the city center. At the bottom of one last hill the SUV bumped over a Rail Canada crossing and abruptly met the river's edge. Conor saw the right-hand turn onto Chemin du Havre just in time. He drove for another mile with only a guardrail between himself and the black, open water of the St. Lawrence on his left.

The port remained hidden until he was almost on top of it. He rounded a curve and came first to a long jetty that served as both a breakwater and scenic viewing point. A few hundred feet farther on, he saw the port itself. As Lucie suggested, it was small and sleepy-looking—just a large, sand-colored warehouse surrounded by a stretch of bare concrete. It was entirely dark except for a few scattered spotlights. These were trained on a container ship snugged up to the edge of the pier, and the name on its prow confirmed it. The Hollumborg had arrived.

Chapter Twenty-Three

THERE WERE ONLY a few cargo containers on board, but even three quarters empty she was impressive, and a bit unnerving to look at. The flat deck resembled a cruise ship stripped down to the waterline, and the towering wheelhouse at the extreme right end gave its entire structure a precarious, unbalanced appearance, as though it might pitch up vertically and sink without a trace. The Hollumborg had cranes fixed at intervals along its length—enormous, sky-scraping arms that looked like they could reach up to a height of twenty floors. Although illuminated by the spotlights on the pier, they appeared immobile.

After parking in an empty lot near the jetty, Conor got out for a closer look, which wasn't very close at all. A flimsy chain-link fence topped with barbed wire surrounded the perimeter of the port. It kept him at a distance, and at an awkward angle. There was also a damp, frigid wind howling over the water, whipping the snow into billowing cyclones that made it hard to see any movement on the pier.

At the main entrance the fence had a sizable gap he could squeeze under, but it didn't seem worth the risk. He returned to the SUV and landed inside, shivering and swearing. Coasting past the port entrance he crossed back over the train tracks and took an immediate left onto an uphill lane. Brightly colored bungalows lined one side, but the river side was undeveloped, providing a clear aerial view of the port. The road dead-ended after a few blocks at a red-trimmed cottage. He looked down and could now see a truck parked near the edge of the pier. Vallencourt's logo was visible on the door, and the nondescript container was still on it.

The cottage looked to be an inn that was closed for the winter, so Conor pulled into its tiny parking lot, positioning himself to face the port, and remained in the Yukon with the heat running. He waited thirty minutes, and was at last rewarded with some movement, not aboard ship, but on the ground. A man appeared from behind the warehouse, crossing the pavement to the container truck.

"There you are. Mounir, is it?" Conor murmured, wishing he had binoculars to see if the face matched Lucie's description.

The man moved swiftly, but stopped at the rear of the truck. He stared at the door with its broken lock, then climbed inside, where he stayed long enough to make Conor wonder if Mounir knew where he was meant to be looking for his prize. He emerged at last, leaping to the ground and running for the ship while signaling up at the silhouette of another figure in the wheelhouse.

It was too far away to hear voices, even if he'd wanted to brave the icy wind of the seaway, but Conor imagined there was a fair bit of shouting going on at this stage. The crane closest to the wheelhouse began rotating toward the pier, its arm slowly bending. As it dipped toward the container truck, he reached for the phone that he'd dropped amid the clutter of the center console.

His report to Reid was short and sweet, and ended just as two sharp raps on the passenger window almost sent him through the roof.

"Mother of—where did you come from?" He squinted at the shape next to the car, too well bundled to identify as man, woman, or child. Again, but more gently, it tapped the window with an ice scraper and then lifted it in a mild salute.

He lowered the window a few inches, nodding a cautious greeting, and got a blizzard of French in response.

"Sorry, I don't understand. I'm . . . American." Conor figured it was close enough and gave a contrite smile.

"Where is Lucie?"

The female voice spoke in English now and the question was clear enough, but he was unprepared for it. Stalling, he opted for stupidity.

"Sorry, what?"

The woman pushed back the scarf wrapped around her head, revealing a rosy-cheeked face framed by a cloud of black, tightly curled ringlets.

"Lucie. It's her car, *non*?" She peered at him. "Who are you?"

"It is her car. Yes. Of course," Conor said, trying to recover. "I'm an old friend of the family, just up for a visit."

He lowered the window further to get a better look at her, confirming an impression that the woman was closer to his own age than Lucie's.

"You're a friend of Lucie's, are you?" Conor asked.

"In a way, yes." She tilted her head, as though considering the idea. "Really it is our husbands who are friends."

"And you live around here?" Conor tried to keep her occupied with his own questions until he could think of how to answer the one that was surely coming.

"Yes, just there." She pointed across the street at a house painted bright blue with yellow trim. "I noticed you a while ago from the kitchen window. What are you doing here in Lucie's car?"

"Ah, well." Conor sighed, rapidly sifting through his options. Since she'd had him under surveillance, the best answer was one that stayed close to the truth. "Lucie wanted to check on the Hollumborg, make sure they got their container back, but she's had a few glasses of wine so I said I'd pop down and have a look. I don't have a car—I came on the train—so I had to take hers." He nodded at the port. The container was now airborne, clutched in the pincer grip of the crane and floating toward the ship. "Looks safe enough,

I'd say. I should be getting back. What's your name? I'll tell her I saw you."

"Yeah, it's Marie. Tell her I said hi. Hey, did Jimmy get back yet? He sounded funny when he called earlier from Magog."

"Did he?" Trying to sound only mildly interested, he took his hand from the gearshift and looked at her again. "No, he's not back. We're wondering what's keeping him. Did he say what he was up to?"

"He said he might go to the casino. He was looking for Gordo—that's my husband—but he's working tonight."

"Ah, I see." A wild exaggeration, because Conor didn't see at all, but after considering another volley of questions, he decided against it. He reached again for the gearshift. "I expect he'll turn up soon, anyway. Nice meeting you, Marie. Best get in out of the cold, right?"

Conor drove off with a backward wave and Marie gave a few more cheery wags of the ice scraper.

"He said he might go to the casino." Repeating her line, Conor barked a laugh at the absurdity of it all.

He tucked the matter into a corner, figuring Lucie could fill in the blanks later about Gordo and Marie, and why her husband might be chancing his luck at the feckin' blackjack tables tonight. It hardly mattered, though. They knew his story now, and wherever the eejit had gone off to, Jimmy wasn't the priority he once had been.

AS LUCIE PROMISED, La Grillade was a restaurant that could not be missed. Conor's bigger challenge was that her Chevy Yukon was too large for the neighborhood street he was navigating to reach it. Running parallel to the main coastal road, it must have been narrow even in summer. Now, the fresh snow piled on either side gave it the width and appearance of a luge run. He inched along within a whisker of parked cars, pulled over to let oncoming traffic pass, and at last arrived at an offbeat structure festooned with wagon wheels. The ones near to the street were half buried in windblown drifts of powder. Instead of a rootin' tootin' frontier town, the scene looked like a snowbound wagon train.

A fenced-in yard stood in front, probably a patio in warmer weather, but stripped of furniture it was more like a corral. A few hardy customers moved around its open area, clutching red Solo cups and never straying far from a wood stove in the middle of it, which had a metallic smokestack shooting a good twelve feet from its top. Beyond the yard was a double-storied porch made of thick, solid timbers, and behind all this camouflage, the facade of the restaurant peeked through, looking modest and residential. A neon sign in flowing script winked coyly next to the front door: *Ouverte.*

Conor backed the SUV into a small parking lot across the street. He felt reasonably certain his man would make an appearance. If Mounir thought he'd been double-crossed, it made sense to start in the place he'd last seen his mark. The next logical move would be a trip to the villa after prying the address out of someone inside. He might not be expecting to find anyone at home, but Mounir would be a fool not to follow whatever leads he had. The biggest unknown was how long it would take him to arrive so Conor could phone in the news and race back ahead of him.

The flames in the woodstove across the street flickered at him like a coded invitation, but it seemed better to wait in the car, and although nobody would recognize him, the street was too narrow and the SUV was too conspicuous to sit idling without drawing attention. He wanted no more encounters like the one with the window-tapping Marie. Conor cut the engine and prepared for a chilly, indefinite vigil in the dark.

He settled back into the leather seat, which for all its softness didn't take long to get cold. He scanned the street to his left, and then to his right; then he peered at a nearby driveway leading to an inn that seemed deserted. Then he returned his gaze to the activity in front of La Grillade, which hadn't changed.

Bored already, he looked at his watch. Ten twenty. He wondered if Kate was still entertaining the gemologist.

"Bloody octogenarian playboy," he muttered, picking up the phone. This time, he entered the private number for their apartment instead of the inn. Lucie's domestic cellular service rejected the call.

"Bollocks." The phone bounced back into the center console, dislodging a half-filled paper cup, but the contents were frozen solid. As he tipped it back into place, he glanced again across the street, and then sat very still.

Beneath the restaurant's freestanding sign, bathed in the light of electric lamps trained on it, two figures stood talking, their heads close together. One of them looked like a heavyweight boxer and the other like the proverbial ninety-eight-pound weakling. The smaller man was trying to shrink even further inside a coat that was no match for the frigid conditions.

"I'll be damned," Conor said softly, recalling T-Dell's description, in all its glorious and accurate detail.

One of those suede jackets the color of baby shit.

Without a doubt, it was Jimmy Denarro.

Chapter Twenty-Four

WATCHING the two men disappear inside, Conor again punched the speed dial for Lucie's home and waited for Reid's laconic greeting.

"Yep."

"I'm parked outside the restaurant. *Jimmy* has just showed up here. He's with a guy who looks like a prizefighter. Has Lucie heard from him at all? Any calls or texts?"

"Not a peep." Reid gave a low whistle. "That's a complication we didn't see coming."

"Too right." Conor popped the door handle, then winced at the blast of arctic air as he hopped from the SUV. "Ask her if she knows who this big fella is—about six three, dark hair in a gelled-up faux hawk, built like a brick shithouse."

After a muffled side conversation, Reid came back on the line. "She says it must be Gordo Powell. He's a forester, but during the winter he works security for the high-rollers salon at the Charlevoix Casino."

"Oh, bloody hell."

Conor felt a growing alarm as the purpose for the casino visit grew clear. Jimmy had apparently decided to try muscling his way out of his troubles, which could prove disastrous for the larger strategy they had in play.

"Look," Reid said, his voice tense. "I think you're going to need to—"

"I know. Already on it." With the clock ticking, Conor kept the call short. "I'll be in touch when I've got something to report . . . one way or the other."

Slamming the phone into his pocket, he took a deep breath to slow his heart rate and assumed a bland expression, then he crossed the street, slipped between two parked cars, and sauntered into the restaurant.

If he had come to La Grillade that night for an evening of western-themed entertainment, Conor would have been disappointed. The interior trimmings certainly promised something along those lines. There was a lot of barn board, and a photo of John Wayne. The place was also strewn with cowboy boots, saddles, and more wagon wheels, plus the horns of several oxen, a few of them strung with multicolored holiday lights, but the poster he'd passed on the porch and his own ears indicated what the patrons were really in for—an evening devoted to the stylings of a Foreigner tribute band called Dirty White Boy. On the floor above, the group had launched into its first set, thumping out their rendition of "Head Games."

There were seating areas to the left and right as he entered, both of which were packed with diners. An enclosed staircase stood opposite the front door, but although Lucie had named the second floor as the main hangout, he scanned the dining room as well. A delicious aroma of charcoal-broiled meat enveloped the restaurant, along with the sweeter scent of baking apples. The decor and overall ambience might be pure kitsch, but judging by the mouth-watering plates Conor glanced at, the food was at another level entirely.

He mounted the worn steps, the music getting louder as he climbed, and emerged into a large, crowded room. Wooden booths lined the walls, their benches padded and covered in red vinyl. In the middle space customers gathered around high-top tables facing the band, which played from an alcove at the back of the building. Its four members—an abridged version of the original—were shifting into "Blue Morning, Blue Day." At a spacious corner bar on the wall opposite the band, Jimmy and Gordo stood with their backs against the counter, gripping pint glasses filled with something dark. Conor watched the band for a few seconds, then crossed the room to edge in next to Jimmy. Along with being slight and bony, he had the sort of shadowed, bloodless complexion that looks best inside nightclubs.

"Is it porter or stout?" He nodded at the glass.

"It's, uh . . . stout," Jimmy said. The accent was American, with a thin, nasal twang. "Milk stout called La Vache Folle."

"The Mad Cow?" Conor grinned. "Interesting choice for a steak house. It's good, though?"

"Yeah, yeah." Jimmy glanced at the sleepy-looking Gordo, who gave an impassive what-can-you-do shrug of his massive shoulders.

There was little point—and very little time—to carry on with the usual protocols for "chatting up strangers in a bar," so Conor didn't waste another minute on them.

"Right. Listen to me, Jimmy, and . . . Gordo." He tilted toward the burly man, whose head snapped around at the sound of his name. "Whatever plan you've hatched up for tonight, I promise you I've got a better one."

With a jerk, Jimmy pitched several ounces of Mad Cow onto the floor in front of him. His eyes grew wide and his lips moved, but the words were lost among guitar chords. Whatever they were, this time Conor had a response ready.

The leather wallet he flipped out of his pocket was one Kate had given him as a joke. The cover was stenciled in gold with the fussy heraldry of the House of Nassau-Weilberg, her family's coat of arms. There were probably less than two hundred people in the world who would recognize it, but it came with all the frills of crowns, banners, and lions rampant. It would look plausible to any citizen of the British Commonwealth, and Conor had known it would come in handy someday. Pivoting to use his body as a shield against curious onlookers, he gave the men a brief glimpse at the exterior, and flashed them a peek at the inside. It was his Green Card, which he disguised by blocking the "permanent resident" label with his finger.

"Special investigations," Conor said. The wallet was in his pocket again before they'd had time to even blink at its details. "We've got the whole story—Mounir, the truck, the diamond, the Marlboro box, the deer. We're up-to-date on all of it, except maybe this High Noon at the Steak House bit. I think it would be better to talk outside."

He addressed the two of them but kept a wary eye on Gordo, not trusting the hibernating bear act, but the bouncer seemed happy to follow Jimmy's lead. He placidly trundled after them once the younger man, even whiter now, agreed to the suggestion.

Ahead of them both, Conor was a few steps down the staircase when on the floor below, he saw the front door swing open. It admitted a gust of frigid air smelling of woodsmoke, and right behind that came the captain of the Hollumborg.

Chapter Twenty-Five

WITH HIS HEAD down and a watch cap pulled low on his forehead, Mounir's facial features were obscured, but the ship's name stitched into the breast pocket of his anorak was a lucky break.

Reversing direction, Conor stopped Jimmy's forward motion with a chest bump. "Back, back, back," he hissed, then lazily started removing his coat, spreading it wide to block the stairwell while his two charges stumbled back on their own tracks.

Turning at the top of the stairs, he faked some friendly horseplay, clapping a hand on Jimmy's shoulder, steering him toward the front of the building. Conor smiled while pitching a question next to his ear.

"Please God that door ahead of us is unlocked?"

He got no answer from Jimmy, but felt a tap on his own shoulder. He turned to see Gordo, who looked more alert now, offering a packet of Viceroys and nodding meaningfully at the door.

"Cheers." Conor took a cigarette and handed the packet forward. "Let's go out for a smoke."

"Fire escape on the left."

These first words from Gordo, delivered with a gravel-bottomed rumble, were music to Conor's ears, but once on the deserted porch he swore, tossing the unlit cigarette over the railing.

While everything else was swept clean on the platform, against all proper regulations the fire escape was invisible under at least two feet of hard-packed snow.

"Hey. Hey, hold on," Jimmy protested, but Conor was already pushing him forward again. At the top of the stairs he swung an arm around Jimmy's chest, gave a kick to the side of his ankle to knock his feet out, and sank back to take the man's slight weight.

"Knees up," he ordered. "Like you're doing a cannonball."

The two of them slid over the edge and shot down the stairs on their backsides. Conor gave thanks for the versatility of a waxed field coat. Landing hard on the plowed driveway, he scrambled up and hauled Jimmy to his feet. Encumbered by size and a pure wool peacoat, Gordo followed more slowly, reaching bottom after Conor had already dragged Jimmy into the deep shadows of a portico in front of the deserted inn next door.

"You did have a plan, I assume," he remarked when they were all together again. He looked at each of them, offering either an invitation to speak while he slapped the snow from his jeans.

"Yeah, I had a great one, so I hope you know what you're doing," Jimmy snapped. "I had it under control."

"By getting Gordo here to give Mounir a good fright? Box the head off him? And then what?"

"Maybe we had a more permanent solution," Gordo said, gazing into the distance. Conor gave him a flat stare, thinking he had vastly underestimated what this hulking lumberjack was bringing to the table.

"You're telling me you were intending to murder the captain of the Hollumborg?" His tone was deadly enough to break the man's impassive self-assurance.

"I didn't say that."

"You didn't have to."

"Well, the guy's—"

"Keep your voice down," Conor snapped at Jimmy.

"The guy's a freakin' criminal," Jimmy whispered. "What were we supposed to do?"

"How about what any half-witted gobshite might do—call the cops?"

Sullen, Jimmy looked away. "I had no proof."

"Because you lost the diamond on a dirt road in Vermont," Conor said.

"*You* lost it?" Gordo stirred like some large animal shaking itself awake. "You said Lucie lost it."

With no answer to give, Jimmy tried shrinking a little further into his shit-brown jacket. Conor swallowed an incredulous laugh.

"What a piece of work you are. Anyway, doesn't matter right now. You're coming with me, and *you* . . ." He swung around to Gordo. "You're going back inside. Do you have a phone?"

"Yeah." Gordo pulled one halfway from his pocket to show him.

"Good, and you know this guy?"

"Mounir? Yeah. I can keep him occupied for a while. Is that what you want?" Gordo was smooth, Conor had to admit that. He'd transferred his allegiance without so much as a glance at Jimmy.

"That's what I want," he said. "He'll be looking for Jimmy, so just tell him you're expecting him to show up"—Conor checked his watch—"say in about half an hour. When he doesn't, I guarantee Mounir will ask for Jimmy's address, and you're going to give it to him. As soon as he leaves, you're going to call the house. You've got that number?"

"Yeah. It's programmed in." Gordo showed the phone again, as if it proved the point. Conor studied him for another fractional moment, hoping he was smarter than he appeared, then with a weary sigh he took Jimmy by the arm and dragged him along to the SUV.

IF ANY QUESTION remained about the precarious state of Lucie and Jimmy's marriage, the reunion scene Conor, Reid, and Nicky witnessed settled it. Once they were again gathered in the kitchen of the couple's hilltop villa, Lucie began shrieking in French about his idiocy and incompetence, and Jimmy railed back in English about her disloyalty and desertion. Each made valid points, and Conor was thoroughly sick of both of them.

While they bickered at the table, he retreated to a spot next to the stove to be near to the pot of vegetable soup Lucie had heated while they waited for his return. Realizing he'd eaten nothing since the pub in Newport twelve hours earlier, Conor inhaled a large bowl of the soup along with six inches of a baguette, and wiped out a plate of vanilla-frosted Christmas cookies for good measure. He gave Nicky and Reid an update between bites.

As for the two officers, they had been filing reports and activating their own networks to dig for information on Mounir, but so far the networks had been slow to respond.

"It's a hard sell," Reid said. "A diamond no one has claimed or seen for a while rattled around in a few odd places and is now safe in the hands of the FBI. Nobody's going to be much interested until there's a better reason to be."

"Yup. Same boat here." Nicky winked at them. "My captain thinks we're being generous enough with our British and American friends by loaning me out to you."

"And he's right," Reid assured her. "We wouldn't be here now without your help."

"We'd have never made it past that moose," Conor added.

"Ha!" Nicky laughed and then lowered her voice to a playful whisper. "Maybe Conor McBride should call up *his* friends."

"At this hour? He'd be annoyed. At this hour on another open line? He'd slaughter me."

He wanted to check in at home, though, and give Kate the latest news as he'd promised. Since they were in a holding pattern and he didn't know when the next opportunity would come, Conor borrowed Reid's phone again, then walked to the den and through the double doors that gave access to the deck. He was glad to be outside again. Now that his stomach was full he'd begun feeling sleepy, but the pure, cold air acted like a splash of ice water to the face. It was also blessedly quiet on the deck. He took a moment to enjoy the peaceful surroundings, letting them put him in the right mood for calling home.

"This is unbelievable," Kate said, once he'd brought her up to speed. Then, as was so often the case, she zeroed in on what was most on his mind. "That Coptic cross. Have you mentioned anything to the others about the vibe you got from Lucie's sketch?"

"That it gave me a shiver?" Conor swept some snow from the deck railing and leaned against it, tiredly rubbing his eyes. "No. It's too vague; I'd sound a freak, but I do think it means something. It'll either come clear or it won't. So, what's your plan for tomorrow? Are you traveling with the FBI to New York? I'm trying not to picture you in the back seat with Aldo."

As he'd hoped, Kate laughed, which was very much what he needed just then.

"It turns out we need to travel separately. I've kept my flight. I'll be going to Harry Winston's on my own and will meet with the FBI later, *because* . . ." She dragged the word out for effect. "Agents Knox and Toomey are driving to New Jersey, first. To Fort Dix. They have to bring Aldo back to prison."

"Back to—*what*?!" Conor straightened, his weariness forgotten.

"Yeah, they didn't tell me that right away. He's doing eleven years at the Correctional Facility. For jewel theft."

"Jesus and Mary."

"Don't worry, I've locked up the silver."

"He's *eighty*, you said?"

"Eighty-two, in fact."

"Well, you can't fault his work ethic, the aul' gaffer."

"It's admirable, in a bizarre sort of way."

It felt good to settle back into their usual banter, and from experience Conor knew they could go on for hours. He huffed a sigh. "I've got to go."

"Okay. I love you," Kate said softly. "I'm trying not to worry, but please be careful, Conor."

"I always am. And to humor the mad, neurotic article who loves *you* something fierce, please take it handy driving to the airport tomorrow."

After ending the call, he continued to linger on the deck, looking at the stars. He had even less appetite now for listening to Lucie and Jimmy snipe at each other, but after a few minutes Nicky was at the door, motioning to him. Gordo was calling.

Chapter Twenty-Six

IN THE LIVING ROOM, Conor picked up the landline phone and right away had to absorb yet another assault on their carefully formed plan.

"I gave him the address, but he's got no car," Gordo said.

Conor sat down on the raised hearth of the fireplace, feeling dwarfed by the edifice of colorful river rocks that took up most of the wall.

"Where are you right now?" he asked. "And where is Mounir?"

"Still at the bar. I'm out on the porch. He wants to use my car. Said I'd have to check with Marie. My wife," he added, sounding sheepish.

"Well done, Gordo. That was very quick thinking." He hoped the dose of praise would make his next directive go down easier. "Now, go back inside and give him your car keys."

"I dunno," Gordo said. "How am I going to get home?"

"Tell him to drop you off. It's on the way."

"You know where I live?"

Conor allowed a ponderous beat of silence to settle over the line before responding. "Yeah. I know where you live, Gordo. Blue house with yellow trim. Listen, mate," he added, sanding the edge off this mafioso moment, "once he gets here this isn't going to take long at all. You'll have it back tonight. I'll drive it down there myself. Okay?"

Gordo reluctantly agreed, and Lucie took his second call less than ten minutes later.

"He's home, and Mounir just left. He should be here in—ahhh!" Her fingers jumped in a spasm of nerves and the phone clattered to the floor.

Nickie fished the handset out from under the sofa and put it back on its cradle. Then, she patted the space above the spiky pink tips of Lucie's hair. "*Calme-toi le pompon.* You are the star of this show. It's no time for stage fright, is it?"

"What show?" Standing at the kitchen table, Jimmy stopped in the middle of pouring himself a shot of Dutch courage from the bottle of Crown Royal. "What are we doing?"

The question brought the rest of them up short. They regarded him as though only now registering his presence. In Conor's opinion, Jimmy's arrival on the scene was not especially welcome. His eyes shifted to his partners.

"Can we use him for anything?"

Nicky squinted at the young man. Her appraisal looked skeptical and obligatory. Reid, already tense and in no mood for improvisation, was shaking his head.

"Not a damn thing. We've rehearsed everything without him; I say we stick to the original script. Just stand over there, out of the way." He briskly dispatched Jimmy to a corner of the unlit den. "You good to go, Lucie? All right. Let's kill the rest of these lights and get into position."

They all fell silent to watch Lucie as she went through the motions of buttoning up the house for the night. First, the brass lamps shining over the deck blinked out, along with the lights on its garlanded railing and those on the Christmas tree inside. Then, the strips of gallery lights trained on the artwork faded to black. Last came the overhead lights and the cozy Tiffany-shaded lamps in the kitchen and living room. When those snapped off, the villa was in darkness. All that remained was a flickering orange gleam of simulated firelight reflecting off the windows. It came from three pillared lanterns placed along the tree-lined path outside. They would serve as the bread crumb trail leading Mounir to the main door in the back.

Conor took up his spot in the den at the eastern end of the house, standing to one side of the only window that faced the road. He kept half his attention focused on the driveway and the other half on Jimmy, who was skittishly hovering a few feet away, near the doors to the deck. Conor gave it fair odds the wanker would bolt through them in a blind panic, at the worst possible moment.

"Come away from the doors." He spoke softly, beckoning him forward as to a cat he meant to coax in out of the rain. Jimmy shuffled a few steps in his direction but couldn't remain still. Fitful, he rocked from one foot to the other until he'd more or less worked his way back to where he'd started.

"Feckin' muppet," Conor sighed.

For a bit of contrast, he looked across the room at Lucie, wondering again how she and Jimmy had ever ended up together. She'd wedged herself into a corner at the bottom of the stairs, and had adopted an expression of fury as an antidote to nerves. She stood as rigid and motionless as the decorative wooden rooster on the floor next to her.

At the other end of the house, he could just see the outline of Nicky tucked behind the edge of the fireplace, facing the back entrance. Her shadowy figure appeared relaxed, but before the last of the lights had gone out he'd seen her hand move to her side and heard the pop and release of the guard on her holster.

Between them both, Reid straddled the kitchen and living areas, just out of sight of the door. His back rested against a load-bearing beam, his service pistol held in a two-handed grip at chest level. They were all in place, with nothing to do but wait.

And wait. After twenty-five minutes the cuckoo clock began its midnight serenade and Reid almost shot it off the wall. It gave them an uneasy sort of comic relief and broke the spell of silence.

"It's only a ten-minute drive from Gordo's house," Conor said.

The obvious follow-up, the question he knew was running through all their minds in some form, remained unspoken. It was rhetorical; unanswerable.

"Maybe he's not coming," Jimmy said, sounding hopeful.

"Maybe," Conor said, but didn't believe it.

A sense of foreboding, rock-hard and insistent, had suddenly fallen like a blow across his back. Something wasn't right, but what was it? Mounir? The plan? One of them? He'd been impatient for the action to start, but now Conor instinctively knew he would run out of time before he could pinpoint the flaw in a setup that was too late to stop . . . and indeed, he did. Less than a minute had passed when a bit of light sliced through a crack in the window's brown silk curtains. He leaned in, leaving them undisturbed, and put his eye to the sliver of space between the panels.

"He's here."

A rustle of fabric and a few creaks from the pine flooring sounded behind him. They were getting ready. Everyone had made some subtle shift of position but Conor remained still, feeling the incipient knot of dread in his back spread from its point of entry, wrapping itself like a vine around every muscle and nerve in his body.

Chapter Twenty-Seven

GORDO'S SILVER Honda swung into the driveway, then disappeared behind Lucie's studio. This was an added wing of the villa that was half its width and extended its length by twelve feet. The driveway beyond the studio couldn't be seen from the rest of the house. Conor had identified this bit of dead ground earlier and tried to eliminate it by putting the SUV there, but there was still space for another car and Mounir had taken it.

Losing the visual was one of the first danger points they'd flagged. If he took the bait, Mounir would be visible again soon, led by the lights down the path to the back door. But he might instead approach the house from the front, and if that happened he'd show up on the deck. They would need to quickly adjust positions to remain hidden. The trick was to move before it was too late, and that was Conor's call.

Although it wasn't loud, he could tell when the engine cut out, but heard no sound of a car door. He stared out the window, focused on the area where Mounir should appear. It was taking too long. Crouched low, he leaned to his right, toward the deck, reminding himself to sweep Jimmy along into the corner and out of sight. He raised a hand, one finger lifting to give the twirling signal to scramble, but then clenched it into a fist. Freeze.

A man had emerged from the shadow of the studio's roof. The body build, watch cap, and anorak all matched. Mounir started down the path to the back door and Conor swung away from the window. He flashed a thumbs-up to the others and had moved to his new mark in the kitchen when the landline began ringing.

They all flinched at the electronic trill echoing through the villa, sounding much louder than when the lights were on. From her corner spot in the living room Nicky had a view of the porch through a side window. She nodded a confirmation that Mounir was there, making the call. They let it ring out, and waited to see what he'd do next. Reid pivoted and peeked around the corner at the door.

"Hello? Anyone home? Jimmy? Lucie?"

The voice sounded younger than Conor expected. It had a soft, rolling accent that didn't sound aggressive, but Mounir had pitched it to carry. It became more strident with the second round of knocking, which then turned to an insistent pounding, rattling the large section of stained glass in the door.

"Jimmy! Lucie! I need to speak with you, please!"

After this appeal, the knocking stopped and the phone began ringing again. Reid pulled back from the corner, gun still gripped at chest level. He faced forward, his mouth set in a grim line, and looked nothing now like the folksy police chief that had wandered into Abigail's kitchen that morning.

Conor understood his dilemma. They had wanted to skip this part. They'd hoped Mounir would say or do something on his own to give the excuse they needed, allowing Lucie and Jimmy to remain at a safe distance while the three professionals took him down. It didn't look like that was going to happen. It looked more like Mounir was beginning to think the house was empty and they couldn't allow that, but Conor had lost any desire to force the action to its next level.

He empathized with the haunted memories and second guesses Reid must be wrestling with; he didn't need the details to be well familiar with the struggle. With his own confidence rattled by the suspicion they'd forgotten something, he wondered if they should consider letting their target escape when Reid settled the issue for both of them. He gave a quick pump of his fist and pointed to the den.

Get Lucie. Time to escalate.

HE DIDN'T KNOW how she would perform, how good her instincts would be; but of one thing Conor was absolutely certain—Lucie Vallencourt needed no coaching in the art of escalation. When he crept back into the den and gave the signal, she shot out of the staircase landing like a sprinter from the starting blocks. Before she could streak past him, Conor grabbed her arm.

"Hey. Take a breath and remember what we practiced. This first." He flicked the switch that lit the staircase, which they'd confirmed could be seen from the back door—a signal that the house was occupied, its residents awake. "Now, just the lamp in the kitchen, dimmed, and don't get too close to the door, right?" Lucie nodded and he gave her arm a light squeeze. "Go on, so. It'll be fine."

He followed her, moving quietly and placing himself in the middle of the kitchen. Apparently afraid to remain alone in the den, Jimmy joined him and hovered, still rocking on his feet. With a half turn, Conor clamped one hand on the back of the man's neck, the other over his mouth. Yanking him forward, he breathed into Jimmy's ear.

"Stop. Feckin'. Fidgeting. Got it?"

His eyes enormous, Jimmy nodded, and he released him. "Good."

The phone had already stopped ringing as Lucie switched on the Tiffany-shaded lamp sitting on the oak buffet. A jewel-toned light threw a dim glow over the living room, leaving the perimeter and entryway in shadows.

"*Qui est-ce?*" She snapped the question as though seething in righteous fury at whoever had woken her.

"Lucie, it's Mounir, from the Hollumborg."

"Mounir? Mounir?! Do you know what time it is?"

"Yes, yes. I'm sorry, but it's about the New York job. There are some problems with . . . loose ends." He stumbled over the phrasing and then rushed on. "I'm afraid it cannot wait. I need to speak to you and Jimmy tonight, so please can I come inside and we will fix it quickly."

"Loose ends? Are you kidding me with this crap?!"

Conor and Reid exchanged a nervous glance. She was off script, and her anger sounded a bit too genuine. Reid made a calming gesture that was impatiently waved away, but she took a deep breath before continuing.

"Okay, *lâ*. Listen. Sorry if there are problems, but Jimmy isn't here. Go look for him in the bars."

"Jimmy is . . . ahhh, I see. You are alone."

The statement carried the dead weight of something final, of a decision reached.

"Like every Friday night, *non?*" Lucie's irritation was more forced now, and Conor saw she was trembling. She wrapped her arms around herself before delivering the line they'd agreed would provoke a reaction.

"Go away, Mounir. I don't have what you are looking for. Or, I mean—" She paused, giving space to the idea that she realized she'd said the wrong thing. "I mean I don't know what it's about, I don't know anything."

The silence felt interminable but was worth the wait. When Mounir spoke again, the soft, pleading tone had vanished. The one replacing it had a deadly edge.

"You don't know anything? Yes, that was our intention. I hoped it was still true, but it's not, is it? I think you know exactly what I'm looking for. Have the two of you gone mad? Did you think I wouldn't check, you silly bitch? Did you think I wouldn't find you?"

"It's lost," Lucie shouted. "We don't have it."

"I believe you are lying, Lucie, but even if you are not, the result will be the same."

The threat unspooled like the lazy fall of a curled whip. Conor was moving while Mounir was still delivering it. He reached Lucie as the door gave way with a crash of breaking glass and splintered wood. This, too, was part of the plan. They expected Mounir to force himself in, had counted on it, but the explosive reality was more than either Lucie or Jimmy could stomach. Conor couldn't tell who was shrieking loudest. He saw Nicky, weapon drawn, step from the shadows of the massive fireplace, and as he swung Lucie away Reid slid forward to fill the space where they'd been, leading with his firing arm.

It was a neat piece of footwork they'd practiced a few times, but Conor got no chance to appreciate it. Something on the deck outside had snagged the corner of his eye—a dense, moving darkness that the moonlight didn't penetrate. Before he even understood what he was seeing, in the seconds before the next earsplitting crash, Conor realized what they'd forgotten. He felt nauseated by his sheer stupidity and the consequences that might follow from it.

He was supposed to be a professional, a trained operative; and yet this simple, childishly obvious contingency had never occurred to him.

Mounir had not come alone.

THE DEAFENING NOISE that came next began with a gunshot that atomized the deck's glass wall. Frozen in the act of shattering, it looked like a piece of modern art, then in a rolling wave it crashed into the villa. The dark mass Conor had glimpsed sharpened into the figure of a man in a balaclava. He leapt through the wall's skeletal remains, scattering shards as he advanced, his gun arm swinging toward the kitchen.

Conor had two people in his orbit needing protection, and knew he couldn't spread himself wide enough to cover both. Unarmed, out of options, out of time, he made the only decision he could.

"Down, get down," he yelled at Jimmy as he whirled away, holding Lucie in a tight embrace.

Speechless and shuddering in his arms, she offered no resistance as Conor spun her around. Pushing her into the aisle space between the cupboards and the kitchen's central island, he folded her down, his body shielding as much of her as he could. Behind him, he felt a rush of movement. Jimmy's terrified scream cut out as a volley of gunfire displaced all other sound, and then ended as abruptly as it had started.

"Clear. You're clear, Conor. Get moving." It was Nicky, her

shout muffled by the ringing, white noise roar in his ears. "I've got this guy covered but Mounir is running back the way he came."

He vaulted up from the floor. "Is he—oh, God."

The chairs around the kitchen table had been shot into kindling, and amid the wreckage, Reid lay facedown on top of Jimmy. Neither was conscious. There was a spreading stain of blood on the knotted pine floor. Conor couldn't tell if it was coming from one or both of them, nor could he stop to find out.

"Shit. Shit. Shit." He fumed in a rhythmic chant, sliding on broken glass and melting snow as he ran. Nicky advanced behind him, her gun trained on the man in the balaclava. He had crumpled to the floor with a shoulder wound that was already swamped in blood. Conor dodged around him, searched briefly for the gun the man had dropped, then gave it up and sprinted out through the shattered doorway.

"Is Mounir armed?" He shouted the question back at Nicky, and got the worst possible answer.

"I don't know."

"Shit," he muttered once more, for good measure.

His ears were clearing now, and he heard Mounir on the opposite side of the villa. They were running in parallel, down its exterior length. As they reached the end of the building the rasping breath and muffled thump of boots grew louder. Conor had no time for any sort of plan, only instincts, and they were telling him not to hesitate, to forget Nicky's uncertain response and the spreading stain on the kitchen floor, to ignore the possibility of being showered in gunfire himself, to simply pump his legs and charge with every ounce of strength.

He cornered his edge of the villa a few steps after Mounir, but the silver Honda sat between them with the driver's side facing Conor. With all forward momentum broken, they pulled up short and faced each other, realizing neither held a weapon.

The driveway was the only route of escape now and Mounir was closer to it, but Conor recovered first. He was just a few paces behind in the long race downhill, and at the end of the driveway he couldn't have stopped if he'd wanted to. Becoming airborne—not entirely by choice—he caught Mounir in a flying tackle that carried them across the road, which was mercifully deserted.

They slammed against the plowed wall of snow on its opposite edge. The road sand had not reached this far, and the plow's blade had scraped a surface that shone like polished marble. Immediately, they began sliding down the steep shoulder. Small avalanches erupted from the banked snow as they rolled and pummeled each other. They'd gone a few hundred feet down the celebrated Route du Fleuve before Conor's boot caught on something. He used the leverage to get Mounir flipped onto his stomach and pinned beneath him.

They lay still, both stunned and gasping, then Conor raised himself to a crouch, keeping one knee on the man's back. The road remained empty, and the moon had climbed high into a frozen, crystal clear sky. It hung there like a piece of stage lighting, giving definition to ice floes on the St. Lawrence, washing the scene with a blue-tinted effect. The silence was broken only by their heaving breaths, billowing from their throats like gouts of smoke, and by the more distant, solitary bark of a dog.

Lights began snapping on in chalets tucked amid trees on the surrounding hillside. Whoever was on emergency dispatch in La Malbaie tonight was about to have an exciting shift. A minute later, a beam of light appeared above them, shining from the end of the driveway. Nicky's stocky, silhouetted figure followed. She swung her flashlight from right to left as she walked.

"Down here." He lifted a hand to wave but needn't have bothered; his voice had cut through the frigid night like a megaphone. She trotted down the middle of the road, pulling the handcuffs from her belt.

"Your partner is dead," she said, as she reached them. Conor's head snapped up and Nicky hitched her breath, appalled by his look of panic. "*Jésu Marie*, I'm sorry, Conor. Not you, or not Reid, I should say. I was talking about Mounir's friend. My shots hit an artery and he bled out; it happened quickly."

He felt Mounir's back grow rigid, then limp, all without making a sound.

"What about Reid? And Jimmy," Conor added. "Are they okay?"

"Jimmy thinks he's dying, but he's fine. Lucie is okay, too. She's looking after Reid, who's not so fine." Nicky passed the handcuffs to Conor. "He got himself in front of Jimmy and took at least one bullet, and maybe hit his head going down. He's still unconscious, but breathing. I radioed for an ambulance."

Conor accepted the cuffs and squeezed them viciously, letting the metal dig in to his frozen hands like a penance. How many more times would other people suffer for the mistakes he made? As though sensing this train of thought, and having none of it, Nicky snapped her fingers at him.

"Hey, hey. We thought this through, all of us, *non?* And all of us missed it. We say here in Québec, *Soyez vite sur vos patins.* Be fast on your skates. Sometimes we are; sometimes not."

He nodded without looking up. The thin wail of a siren sounded somewhere below them, growing gradually louder.

"You want to know what I think?" Nicky stopped, waiting until he'd glanced at her. "I think you skate faster than most, Conor McBride; but it isn't always about you, *là.* Don't keep the stupid all for yourself. Sometimes you have to share it."

Conor smiled at this bit of practical wisdom, appreciating the unflappable, generous heart of the woman delivering it. He took a lungful of air and coughed on a short laugh.

"An Irishman on skates. You haven't a *notion* of the comic potential in that. You win, Nicky Simard. We are a pure shower of eejits, then, all of us. I'm just praying it won't matter too much."

Nicky nodded. "Me, too."

"And for the cherry on top, I've never worked a pair of these in my life." He tossed the handcuffs back to her. "I'll do the heavy lifting, will I? And you can have the glory."

He removed his knee from Mounir's back. Sensing no resistance or struggle, he took a firm but not brutal grip on the man's arms, pulling first one and then the other into position. He shifted to give Nicky an opening for the handcuffs, breathing in the arctic air more carefully this time. The exhale locked in his throat, then released in a gust. Conor stared at the man's right wrist, and angled it for a better look. Captured in a shaft of the moon's ice-blue spotlight, the dark outline of a tattoo leapt into focus. A Coptic cross.

Chapter Twenty-Nine

HE'D BEEN inside plenty of hospitals, in both a voluntary and involuntary capacity. He had no complaints for their customer service, but Conor thought St-Joseph de la Malbaie might be in a league of its own. With Reid as the main attraction, he expected no attention at all, but while the chief was being evaluated and wheeled around the place from MRI to X-Ray, an ER nurse spent more time on Conor than he felt worthy of receiving. A gash on his chin that he hadn't even noticed received impeccable treatment, including four stitches. The surprising amount of blood that had soaked into his shirt got swiftly erased with a miracle cleaning agent. A hospital aide who behaved like a concierge guided him to a comfortable waiting room, floated away, and returned with a plate of biscuits on a tray and a pot of tea that was actually drinkable. Nicky had booked him at a luxury hotel in town called Le Manoir Richelieu. He doubted they could top St-Joseph's five-star service.

His only point of concern was how often passing staff members asked if he was all right, or if he would like to lie down for *une petite sieste*. Once he'd faced himself in the men's room mirror, he better understood their worry. He looked tired, unshaven, and disheveled, and apart from the chin was feeling the effects of fighting bare-handed in subzero weather while bouncing hundreds of feet down a rock-hard road. Nicky added to the chorus when she arrived an hour later and sank into the chair next to him.

"You should be in bed."

"Probably," Conor concurred. "Nicky, how is it you never mentioned I was bleeding like a stuck pig?"

She looked surprised. "You didn't know? I thought you were being a tough guy. Come, I'll take you to Le Manoir. I just spoke to the doctor and she said Reid will be fine. One bullet only—a shot to the knee—and a concussion."

"Yeah, I saw her too, a few minutes ago."

They were still waiting for test results on the knee, which Conor had seen and thought was shattered, but thankfully the concussion wasn't severe, and the doctor expected Reid to wake soon. He had an inkling what that would be like, surfacing after a shoot-out you hadn't seen the end of—the rise from a black, dreamless void; the confusion of memories, trying to sort new ones from those years gone by; and the panic that lands like a punch to the gut when you realize the memory you're reaching for and the thing it represents isn't there. You don't know yet if you've failed again. You won't, until someone tells you.

"I'll stay awhile. Just until he comes around."

Remembering that Nicky was likely dealing with heavy thoughts of her own, Conor swiveled to face her. "You saved all our lives tonight. When I first ran past that guy in the balaclava, I figured we'd been lucky you hadn't missed entirely. It was a lot of blood for a shoulder wound but it didn't seem like a kill shot. I took another look when we got back. Two wounds, on either side. Two carotid arteries. That kind of aim takes years of practice, but I'm guessing you never believed you'd have to kill a man with it."

"No. I didn't." The hitch of emotion in Nicky's voice was unreadable on her face. "And I hope that will be the last. It's not why I joined the RCMP."

"Are you okay?"

"Right now? I'm fine. Like you, *eh?*" She shot him a look full of understanding about things he had not told her. "Most of the time, we're fine."

"Fair enough." He backed off, knowing better than most when to stop prying. "Tell me what's happening on your end. And sorry, by the way, for taking off in the ambulance. It feels like I left you with the washing up."

Nicky shook her head. "*Pas de tout*. It's best we leave you out of it, *non?* Lucie and Jimmy are also at Le Manoir with an RCMP detail so they won't get lonely. They'll be questioned later. Mounir is going to Québec for a start. He's made not one peep so far. There are dozens of texts on his phone but we can't make sense of them. The words didn't connect with anything in the translation software."

An idea struck Conor. As a product of Ireland's Irish-speaking Gaeltacht, he knew how to use an obscure language for secretive purposes.

"I wonder is there a Coptic language?"

"Ahh." Nicky looked thoughtful. "Why not? It's worth trying. That tattoo on Mounir's wrist. You saw the same on Mr. Balaclava?"

"I did. Have you identified him?"

"Not yet, but he surely came from the Hollumborg. The Coast Guard has secured the ship and will interview everyone on board, but this Coptic cross business is tricky, Conor. Okay, maybe it becomes important later, but in the meantime, to investigate everyone's religion? *Non*. It's profiling."

"Understood. It might not mean anything. A few criminals working together share a religion. You can hardly call that a weird coincidence, and we can't really . . ." He trailed off, forgetting whatever point he was going to make. He didn't believe his own argument, and from Nicky's expression it seemed she didn't either.

"I agree. Frustrating. It will be one of the MSETs that takes over from here."

"What's an MSET?" Conor asked.

"Maritime Security Enforcement Team. Units from RCMP

and the Coast Guard. It's their show, now, but . . ." Her grin was pure, mischievous conspiracy. "I know those guys, okay? We'll share with you if you do the same. How does that sound?"

"Sounds like a deal, but let's not share the stupid this time, right?"

Nicky's hoot of laughter made the nursing station staff jump in unison. "Okay, okay, Conor McBride. We can leave that part out." She picked up her hat from the seat next to her and got to her feet. "Now, I should return to Sherbrooke and my paperwork. You'll be here another night or two?"

"At least, yeah," he said. "We'll see what the doctor says. That knee . . ."

"It's a mess. He'll need surgery. Most definitely. No trip to New York, after all." Nicky pulled a frown that was only half-serious.

Of course, she was right. There was no way he could head for home now and leave Reid behind to fend for himself, concussed and alone. He thought about his phone conversation with Kate a few minutes earlier, when he'd delivered the latest news.

"You've every reason to be giving out yards to me," he said into an unearthly silence. "I should have started back yesterday after-noon instead of swanning off into the Canadian wilderness."

Kate released a gusty sigh. "Except someone might have ended up dead if you hadn't been there."

"Maybe you're wishing I had, at this stage."

"Stop it."

"You aren't angry?" Conor said, then braced himself for what-ever would follow such an idiotic question.

"Of course I'm angry!" Kate snapped. "Just . . . not with you, which is extremely frustrating, because I need to be 'giving out yards' to somebody, dammit. I want to be furious with you, but you're doing the right thing, and I can't be mad at Reid after he's been shot saving Jimmy's life, and—Jimmy. Jimmy Denarro is who I'd take a slice from if I got the chance; why did he have to be such an idiot?!"

"Many here would like to know as well," Conor said. "Including his wife."

It was odd how crushed he felt about missing an event he'd been dreading for weeks. Seeing his glum expression, Nicky grew more serious and gave him an affectionate punch on the shoulder.

"Hey. Don't waste time moping, okay? You need to think how you'll make it up to her. Keep in touch; tell me know how it goes, *eh?*"

"I will." He rose and they stood facing each other uncertainly, until Conor cocked an eyebrow and smiled. With another booming laugh, she embraced him in a crushing bear hug.

"Come back sometime with Kate. My Édouard is a chef in Sherbrooke, you know. He'll cook for you, real food *à la Québecois.*"

"I'd like that. I'd love it, in fact. Eating is my particular specialty."

"Mine too. It's obvious, *non?*! Ah! I almost forgot. When you are ready, the RCMP here in La Malbaie can drive you as far as Québec City. From there it's up to you how to get back to the border and your squad car."

"We'll figure something out," Conor said. "Safe home, Nicky, and thanks. For everything."

Okay. *A bientôt* my friend."

"*A bientôt.*"

As she headed down the hall, he added, "*Soyez vite sur vos patins.*"

"It's good, it's good! You're a quick learner." She gave a final wave with the beaver fur hat and disappeared out the door.

Chapter Thirty

IT WAS NEARLY four in the morning. Shifts were preparing to turn over and there were more call buttons sounding, more trollies and trays in the hallway, the occasional bloom of noxious odors quickly deodorized. The activity level was working toward rush hour, but it had never really been quiet. Conor had been dozing in a reclining vinyl chair, but sounds of agitated movement snapped him to attention. Reid was still not awake, but his eyes moved rapidly under closed lids, twitching as if in the grip of a dream, or nightmare. Leaning on the bed rail, Conor coaxed him the rest of the way.

"Reid. Wake up now, mate. You're all right. It's okay."

As though coming up through water, he surfaced with a sobbing gasp. He stared at him without recognition, his eyes full of wild questions, and tried to vault up from the bed. Conor was ready for this and kept him in place with a firm but gentle pressure.

"Where are they? Where? Where are—" The question cracked apart from the effort of forming it and Reid frowned, as though trying to remember what he was asking, who he was looking for. "What happened? Where are they?"

"Safe and well." He enunciated for clarity. "All of them. Everyone is safe and well."

"It's, it's—" Reid's painful contortions ended in a long sigh. "Guy named Jimmy. Jimmy with the diamond. Jimmy the, the—"

"The plonker who dumped us into this shite." Conor gave him a broad grin. "Welcome back to the world, Marshal Briggs."

Reid peered up, recognizing him this time. "Conor," he said, his voice weak. "He's okay? Injuries?"

"Not a scratch. You laid him flat and covered him like a rug. *He* is having a good kip for himself at the fanciest place in town, while *you*"—he positioned a cup of water under the man's chin and popped the straw into his mouth—"while you are sucking on a straw in the St-Joseph de Malbaie ER, and c'mere, probably getting better service."

After draining the cup twice, Reid looked more alert as he settled back against the pillows. "You look like hell."

"Yeah, I've seen that, thanks. Shall I fetch the mirror for you, now?"

Reid's laugh became a grimace, and Conor joined him in it.

"Sorry. And be careful there," he added, as the patient began to stretch. "There's a shattered knee, I'm told. They're going to admit you as soon as they've got a bed free."

"Yup, found it," Reid hissed. "Damn. Any more good news?"

"The tea here is outstanding." Conor snorted at his own joke then rubbed his face. "Jaysus. I'm a little punchy, I guess. It's four o'clock in the feckin' morning, after all."

"I should let you get some sleep," Reid said. "I'd be grateful for the debrief first, though. Could you fill me in before you go?"

Conor smiled. "I'd be only delighted."

It didn't take long to color in the picture for Reid. The action had been rapid and intense after he'd been shot, but it had also been soon over. He had moved on to the latest information—the messages found on Mounir's phone—when, as if on cue, a hospital volunteer bustled in saying Nicky had phoned. She was on hold at the nursing station waiting to speak with him. When Conor greeted her, Nicky's full-bodied voice shouted down the line.

"*Oppeulaille!* You were correct, my friend! The texts are in

Coptic. We woke one of our CSIS language analysts and emailed screenshots. She recognized it and found a translator already vetted through their academic program. Now, we know a lot more, and if we are lucky? We will have at least another person in custody by this afternoon."

"That's fantastic, Nicky. Ehm, hang on, though." Although eager for details, Conor was noting the hospital volunteer's mild look of reproach. "The nursing staff wants their phone back and Reid is awake now. Just give me a tick to run over to his room and then call his mobile. You can update us both at the same time."

A few minutes later, Reid's phone sat on a tray table between the two of them. They needed no speaker function. With the volume at its normal level, they could easily hear Nicky summarize the translated messages from Mounir's phone.

The tone and substance of the texts made it clear Cyril was in charge. He delivered the orders and Mounir saluted. In their exchanges, they referred to the diamond as "the container," and the earliest communications dealt with the logistics and urgency of getting it from New York to Canada, and then to Egypt. After its port call at Pointe-au-Pic on Friday evening, the Hollumborg would head for the Port of Alexandria, arriving in five days with the Star of the East aboard, stowed in the captain's safe.

"Anything about the logistics for Cyril getting hold of 'the container' in the first place?" Reid asked. Although still groggy and clearly in pain, the discussion seemed to give his spirits a boost.

"Nothing," Nicky said. "Either he already had the diamond, or knew how to get it."

She described a series of messages about hiring and paying Jimmy as an unwitting accomplice. Tuesday evening, Cyril confirmed Jimmy and Lucie's arrival at Red Hook Terminal, and texted again when they left on Thursday with the diamond hidden in their truck.

"Everything was going according to plan until yesterday morning. Mounir sent a text saying 'Problem. Routing update with two-week delay.' Right after, the phone log shows they had a five-minute call."

"Do we have any way of knowing what that meant?" Conor asked.

"*Bien sûr.*" Nicky's voice grew excited again. "The Coast Guard confirmed the ship had new orders and would reverse course after its stop at Pointe-au-Pic. Instead of heading to the Atlantic and on to Alexandria, Mounir's new route would go back down the St. Lawrence and into the Great Lakes. In their phone call, Cyril must have come up with a plan for Mounir to transfer the diamond to a courier. Mounir sent a final text yesterday afternoon. It reads 'Tell courier tomorrow 1500h. HB bar.' A few hours later, Cyril replied 'Done,' and that was their last communication. *Et voilà!*" She finished on a note of triumph.

"This is bloody good work, Nicky," Conor said. "You've got a sound team of spooks working in Ottawa. That's three o'clock this afternoon. Have you identified the location for Mounir's meeting with the courier? Where was the Hollumborg meant to be at three o'clock today?"

"The Coast Guard is getting an update of the route from the shipping company. When we know the port, it should be easy to identify any bar with the initials 'HB.' Since that was the last time they communicated, Cyril doesn't realize Mounir is in custody. We hope the courier will turn up as planned and the RCMP will be there to make the arrest."

"Interesting that it's a *courier*." Reid drew the word out thoughtfully. "I wonder who that will be, and whether the assignment is to bring the diamond back to Cyril in New York or get it to Egypt?"

"That was my question as well," Conor said. "Feels like we're stuck in some banjaxed treasure hunt with the clues out of order and the prize found at the beginning."

"They may be out of order, but the clues are carrying us forward," Nicky said. "I need to get on the road now. I was halfway to Sherbrooke but have turned back toward the coast, hoping to reach the meeting point in time once we identify it. I should phone the hospital room's number with updates, *oui?*"

"*Bien sûr.*" Conor tried to sound cheerful for Reid's sake. "Neither of us is going anywhere."

Chapter Thirty-One

WHEN A TAXI DROPPED him at the entrance of Le Manoir Richelieu, Conor was startled to see its style was far more French chateau than cozy manor house. The place was immense—a copper-roofed, granite fortress sitting on a high bluff above the St. Lawrence. On the extensive grounds in front of the hotel, old-fashioned streetlamps, decked with garlands and holiday wreaths, threw discs of light onto an Olympic-sized skating rink. Beyond it, the hillside rolled down to the cliff's edge, where a stone parapet formed the boundary for a winding promenade.

The setting offered a dramatic, panoramic view to the east, where the river widened as it approached the Atlantic. The night was slow in surrendering its winter darkness, but Conor noted the moon had set, and the sky in that direction was turning a light shade of violet.

Climbing a staircase inside the main entrance, he ascended to a vast, colonnaded hall sprinkled with leather couches and chairs in quiet alcoves. The dark wood floor and oak-beamed ceiling carried a whiff of oil soap, and dimly lit chandeliers created a sense of permanent twilight. The overall effect was a sort of medieval elegance.

Apart from a faint clatter of silverware there were no other signs of life, but halfway down the hall, tucked behind a twelve-foot Christmas tree wrapped in a swirling, red velvet ribbon, he found the reception desk and its one lonely attendant.

Conor pocketed his key after checking in, discovering he'd somehow lost the appetite for sleep. He was more interested in breakfast, but the dining room wouldn't open for another hour. He didn't know what time Kate was leaving for her flight to New York, but thought it was too early to call her. He had learned it was almost never a good idea to wake her, and if up, she was probably running behind, because she always set her alarm with hilarious delusions about her own efficiency. Some of his best entertainment came from watching her mad scramble around their bedroom.

With no brain power left for creative thinking, he went back outside and walked a few laps along the cliffside promenade. Feeling better for the exercise, he wandered across the parking lot to an adjacent building getting an unusual amount of foot traffic, and soon discovered he'd stumbled upon Gordo's place of work: the Charlevoix Casino.

Conor made a tour of the gaming salon. His boots sank into plush carpeting, soft enough to sleep on if his interest in it returned, and he counted more people than he would have expected to find there before dawn on a Saturday morning. A staff member explained a poker tournament was underway, and this led to the discovery of a restaurant that was on a twenty-four-hour schedule for the weekend.

The tea fell short of the St-Joseph benchmark, but the breakfast poutine made up for it. The fried egg over a mound of hand-cut french fries soaked in brown gravy and cheese curds was a heart-stopping revelation. He almost wished he had the hangover it would most certainly cure.

As he was paying the bill, Lucie's phone came alive with a vibrating ring inside his jacket. He'd forgotten it was still there. Conor fumbled it out of his pocket and heard Reid's voice on the line when he answered.

"Sorry, Conor. Did I wake you?"

"No, I decided to eat instead." He accepted his receipt from the cashier with a wink. "What's the story? Missing me already?"

"I just had a visit from the doctor. The leg needs emergency surgery. They want to ship me down to Quebec City by ambulance."

"Damn. When's that happening?"

"Well, it's not." Reid cleared his throat. "I told them I'm not going."

Conor started back through the casino, heading for the front door. "Ohhh-kay. Because . . . ?"

"Look, the people here are wonderful. I've never met any better. They've been friendly and kind, and—"

"Canadian. They've been very, very Canadian. The stories are true—to their enormous credit—but you don't trust the surgeons."

"I'm not saying I don't trust them," Reid protested. "I'd just trust someone else more."

"You've someone else in mind?"

"The guy who did the *other* damned knee. It's not my first trip to the rodeo, Conor; I've already got a leg that's three parts titanium. Hello? I think the signal's going. Can you hear me?"

"I can. Just . . . hang on a minute."

Conor lowered the phone. He was laughing too hard to say more. The deer, the diamond, a moose, that feckin' beaver hat, an eighty-year-old jewel thief, and a US Marshal with a bionic knee, looking for a second one. If life were fair, he'd dine out on this story for years and never have to buy another drink. He sat down at a slot machine and collected himself.

"Sorry, Reid. Signal seems good now. We'll cut straight to the point, will we? I'll figure the rest out; just tell me where I need to get you."

"New York City. Mt. Sinai."

Conor gazed in dreamy speculation at the machine in front of him—the Triple Diamond, naturally—and felt the wheels spin inside his own head. "New York. That works for me."

"I was hoping it would." He heard the relief in Reid's voice.

"We can wait until after three o'clock if you want to see what happens with this courier."

"Feck the courier," Conor said, with absolute sincerity. "The MSETs are in charge now, which means whatever half-arsed story Fr—" He swallowed the name in time to avoid identifying his MI6 superior. "What I mean is, I don't need to be here anymore, and Nicky can call your mobile with updates. Sit tight another little while. I'll get us out of this place as quick as I can."

After ending the call, he sat thinking for a minute, remembering the sign he'd passed on the road pointing to the Charlevoix Regional Airport and calculating what hour it was on the Vistula Spit, and what Frank might be doing right now. Lucie's phone had no international service, but he couldn't have used it, anyway, and the one in his hotel room wasn't an option either.

It was partly Frank's fault he was still in Canada at all, but Conor knew it was a big ask he was thinking about—the mother of all favors. He had to be a good little spy this time.

After placing another call on Lucie's phone to get the advice he needed, he found the high-rollers salon and approached the muscular bouncer who was guarding the door.

"Jerome, is it? How's it going, there. I was just talking to my buddy Gordo, and he says you're the man who can set me up with a burner phone."

Chapter Thirty-Two

CONOR'S TUXEDO was hooked on the bathroom door, and Kate had flown past it several times while packing, swearing at herself for getting behind schedule. She'd almost left it hanging there, but after throwing everything else into the car, she ran back inside to grab it.

"You never know," she said, zipping it into the garment bag. "He's been known to surprise me before."

A few minutes earlier, FBI agents Knox and Toomey had departed with Aldo. At first, they'd insisted they would get break-fast en route; but Aldo looked so glum at this prospect that Kate didn't have the heart to hold back a last burst of hospitality. She whipped up some pancakes and bacon and accepted accolades from her admirer that went well beyond what the meal deserved.

With time running short, she had hurried the elderly man into his enormous down jacket. It only made him look smaller, and more forlorn. She cheered him up with a kiss on the cheek and assur-ances he would always be welcome at the Rembrandt Inn, saying she hoped he would return whenever . . . well, whenever he could.

Worried about the hours they'd lose processing Aldo back through the prison system, the agents agreed to let Kate make a private appointment with Harry Winston's and bring the diamond with her. They planned a meeting for four o'clock at a Yorkville diner near her grandmother's apartment.

Once underway, she focused on making up for the late start. By nature, combined with recent, unconventional training, she'd developed a style of driving Conor described as "three parts genius, one part demented." He'd resigned himself to a copilot role for most of their road trips, and, if asked how the drive was when they arrived, often replied, "lively."

This morning, with the roads sanded and dry, Kate made the most of her talents. She always hoped to arrive at the airport in Burlington with time to enjoy a cup of coffee before calmly walking to her gate, but, as usual, this was not one of those days. She rocketed over the skyway from the parking garage to the terminal and was thankful to at least not be the last passenger boarding.

In the window seat of the cramped, two-seater row, Kate was careful not to encroach on the one next to her, until she remembered Conor should be sitting in it. With a sigh, she dropped her coat onto the empty seat and opened the magazine her stepmother had mailed to her—*Sophisticated Weddings: The Jamaica Edition.*

Her flight landed at LaGuardia just before nine o'clock. After locating and settling into the black sedan her grandmother had sent for her, Kate phoned Harry Winston's flagship salon on Fifth Avenue to request an appointment. She wanted to keep the purpose of her visit vague, and would name-drop if needed, but none of that was necessary. Her call was transferred to the salon manager, a woman named Phoebe Long, who sounded middle-aged and oddly distracted. Without collecting any information—not even Kate's name—she confirmed her availability.

"Certainly, I'll be happy to meet you. Delighted. The salon is open until eight this evening, and I'll . . . well yes, of course I'll be here until eight, too. Come anytime. Yes, noon, that's fine. Thank you so much. Looking forward. Mmm. Mmm. Mmm-hmm."

After these few bars of agitated humming, the call ended without another word. Kate took the phone from her ear and looked at it to confirm the line was dead.

"Interesting," she murmured, but then thought she might be making too much of the woman's manner, seeing a connection to their mystery where none existed. Maybe she was simply running behind schedule. Kate could sympathize with that.

She tapped a fingernail a few times against the armrest, which sounded loud in the regal, monastic hush of the sedan. The driver glanced in his rearview mirror and she flashed a guilty smile, as if she'd been caught scratching her name into the back seat. He gave a quick answering grin, a reassurance that he wasn't being weird about the upholstery. She considered starting a conversation, but that only reminded her again of Conor, who would certainly have plunged into one by now. If he were here. With her. She turned to the window, relieved her driver wasn't a talker. Kate didn't feel like chatting and didn't care what he thought about it.

She did appreciate the skill of his driving. He'd expertly cut through the morning rush hour traffic, and sooner than she'd expected they were on the Upper East Side, turning off FDR Drive into Yorkville. Here, in one of the last tree-lined neighborhoods in the city, her grandmother, Sophia, had lived for the past forty-five years.

SOPHIA'S PENTHOUSE apartment was on two floors at the top of an eclectic pre-war building. An open-air terrace surrounded three sides of it and offered breathtaking views of the East River. She'd shared the home with her husband, William Bunting, until his death eight years earlier. Since then, she'd been fending off suggestions from Realtors—and even a few neighbors—that she would be more comfortable in a smaller space, on a lower floor.

Those who'd lived longest in the building remembered William as a shy but friendly physicist. Most never knew he was also heir to a fortune made from refrigeration patents. Speculation about how he afforded a penthouse residence on an academic salary had fueled cocktail party gossip for years.

"I told Wim this was his greatest act of chivalry," Sophia once said. "He endured the spotlight and shielded me."

Even now, with her husband gone, most tenants knew her only in passing, a petite, charming neighbor with silvered red hair she wore back in a loose but tidy knot. She had a residual accent they found hard to place, and a manner of posture and fashion that belied her eighty-one years.

It amused Kate that only a handful of the old guard understood her full name to be Princess Sophia Alexandra Ingrid Marie, a member of Luxembourg's Royal House of Nassau-Weilburg and the Bavarian House of Wittelsbach. The princess preferred to remain an enigma. She was an active but discreet philanthropist, keeping a low profile and making no apologies for it.

"It makes for tedious conversation," she'd explained to Kate. "People are eager for fairy tales of castles and fancy dress balls, but what can I tell them? I was born between two wars. The first led to abdication and the second to exile and internment, but nobody wants to hear about the sufferings of royalty. Who can blame them? It sounds ridiculous."

Like its owner, the apartment had a casual elegance, its beauty warm and approachable, especially during the Christmas season. As it did every year, Kate's heart soared as she stepped from the elevator's private landing and saw the annual transformation was right on schedule. Her grandmother decorated early, inspired by childhood memories of Christkindlmarkt, a centuries-old tradition that, during the four weeks of Advent, turned her beloved Bavarian city into a festive winter market.

In the large, marble-floored entrance gallery, Kate stopped to breathe in the swirling, evergreen fragrance. Under Sophia's curation, this space never achieved the cold majesty its architect might have intended, and at the moment the gleaming floor seemed more like the snow-covered ground of an enchanted forest. The centerpiece was a Christmas tree standing within the semicircle of the hall's staircase. Twinkling with fairy lights, it soared up to a shining crystal star at its peak. Along the walls, a border of red and white poinsettias created a whimsical candy cane effect.

Growing up, Kate had spent a lot of time in this apartment. She knew her own love for Christmas had been nurtured here and nowhere else. She was the youngest of six children, and almost certainly the least expected. Her birth had ended her brother Peter's five-year reign as the baby of the family. She'd also arrived close to the collision point of unhappy, related events: her mother's death within a year of Kate's birth, and her father's quick adoption of bachelor habits incompatible with family responsibilities.

If not for the love, comfort, and stability of her mother's parents, Kate knew she might have given in to the self-absorption—and self-destruction—that prevailed in the upper-class circle she'd nearly been trapped inside.

Kate heard footsteps from above, and looked up to see her grandmother descending the stairs.

"Hi, Oma. You've made Christmas look amazing, as usual."

Sophia peeked at her through the lower branches of the Christmas tree, her face brightening in a warm smile as she swept down the last few steps.

"Ahh, it *is* you. I wasn't sure if it was the elevator or the cat swatting at the sleigh bells again. Where is Conor?"

Kate was grateful for the hug that hid her face. She had to stop worrying about the party that evening, and about arriving with no fiancé at her side. Far better not to mention it, or think about it, just yet. She'd wait until the last possible moment, and, if it came to the worst, let a few stiff drinks see her through.

"There was something he needed to do first. I have a few errands to run, myself," she continued. "I just stopped in to drop off the luggage, and see you."

Sophia pulled back and gave her a searching look. "He's angry with me, isn't he? About the wedding?"

"Oh, God, no. You're about the only one he wasn't angry with in all this. To be honest, Oma, we were both upset for a while, with each other and everyone else. I know they're trying to get a return on investment from this resort, but having Johno and Peter tell us where our wedding will be is outrageous."

"Yes. I've been thinking ever since that I made a terrible mistake. I should have asked Johno more questions, but when he said Peter would be in trouble—"

Kate caught her grandmother's hands and gave them a squeeze. Peter drank too much and gambled too much and was always in trouble, and her brother Jonathan had known Sophia's protective instincts would carry the day.

"It's fine. We're getting used to the idea, and our friends up in Vermont are thrilled to be going to Jamaica." Kate didn't add that she and Conor were covering the travel costs for all of them. "Now, I smell cinnamon, and if that means there is fresh-baked Zimtsterne in this house, I demand to be taken to it."

Sophia led the way to the stairs. "Not just Zimtsterne. There is also Nusstaler, and Spitzbuben, and . . ."

As the litany of Bavarian Christmas cookies went on, Kate groaned in anticipation and followed with a lighter step. Thanks to her grandmother, it was beginning to feel like Christmas. Once that sort of magic takes hold, she thought, anything might be possible.

Chapter Thirty-Three

THE SECOND LEVEL of the penthouse had a library flanked by the master suite on one side and two additional bedrooms on the other. The suite, facing the East River, included a sitting area and a breakfast nook with coffee-making supplies. From there her grandmother sipped her first cup of the day while watching the sun rise.

The coffee itself was a special grind shipped from a roaster in Vienna, but Kate thought the old-fashioned percolator her grandmother preferred was the secret to its excellence. The room soon filled with a rich, dark aroma as the pot bubbled with the signature sound of Kate's childhood.

Sophia placed a large plate of Bavarian cookies on the coffee table, then sat next to her on the sofa, and Kate thought about how to move their conversation in the direction she wanted. Her grandmother knew nothing of the more dangerous aspects of Conor's life, and by association her granddaughter's. Kate didn't mind keeping the rest of her family in the dark, but she hated deceiving Sophia. She'd been wearing down Conor's reluctance, but even if he'd agreed to let her share their secrets, this was hardly the right time to start.

Judging from her last phone call with him, what had begun as an amusing adventure had grown into a darker, more dangerous mystery. If she described the previous twenty-four hours in detail it would lead to a wider discussion she needed to avoid, but Kate wanted to explore Peter's story of meeting Harry Winston in this apartment. If it had happened, it seemed likely Sophia would remember.

Happily, once they'd settled on the sofa, she realized the simplest method for raising the topic was both natural and completely true.

"We had an unusual guest at the inn last night," she said. "A gemologist who specializes in diamonds. He talked about some of the famous ones he's seen and it made me think of a story Peter once told me. He said Harry Winston came here one day when we were kids and showed us a huge diamond that he pulled out of his pocket. Peter says I don't remember because I was only about three. Is it true?"

"It is!" Sophia's smile was wistful and affectionate. "He and his wife, Edna, were here for cocktails. That was just a few years before he died. It was the Star of Independence he had in his pocket, that time. He had it made for the Bicentennial."

"*That* time?" Kate said.

"It wasn't unusual, apparently. Edna said he often carried jewels around in his pockets, and that Lloyds of London often threatened to cancel his life insurance."

"It sounds like you were good friends. Did you get together a lot for cocktails and parties?"

"Not parties, no. They were thirty years older than us, after all. We were friends with Jeff and Marion Winston. Jeff was a favorite nephew of Harry's, and the six of us would sometimes get together. I think we were all going to a play on that night Peter remembers."

"Did he ever show you a diamond called the Star of the East?" Kate focused on selecting another sugar-dusted, jam-filled tart. She hoped the conversation sounded casual. "Our guest said it used to be worn on the same necklace as the Hope Diamond. I guess it belonged to Harry for a while, but now nobody seems to know where it is or who owns it."

"He liked talking about the Hope Diamond, but the Star of Independence was the only one he showed us, and that was enough." Sophia laughed. "Peter ran onto the terrace with it and Wim chased after him. I was terrified the thing would go right over the edge, but Harry thought it was great fun. I did see the Hope Diamond once at the Met—a gala exhibition, several years after both Harry and Edna had died."

"Oh! Aldo—the gemologist, mentioned that event." Kate remembered him saying it was the last time anyone had seen the Star of the East in public. She wasn't surprised her grandmother would only remember the famous gem that always overshadowed it. "It must have been a spectacular night."

"We didn't particularly enjoy it," Sophia said, drily. "Harry's sons Ron and Bruce were fighting over the business and a lot of friends at that event had chosen sides. Terribly awkward for Jeff. It became an open war between the two, with lawsuits that went on for years. Your father played a small role in bringing the feud to an end."

"*My* father?" A stream of coffee swerved toward the rim of Kate's cup. She recentered the percolator in time to avoid a spill. "What did Daddy have to do with it?"

"Several years ago—at one of these ridiculous holiday parties, actually—he introduced Jeff to a partner in a private equity firm. Jeff passed the connection on to Ron Winston, and the firm invested enough to allow him to buy out his brother and put an end to the lawsuit."

"Huh." Filing the information away, Kate looked up from her cup and gave Sophia a conspiratorial smile. "I guess it's nice to know these parties are good for something."

An hour later, fortified with cookies and strong hot coffee, she left for her noontime meeting at the jewelry store. Whenever possible, Kate preferred traveling to Midtown on foot, and a glance at the clock in the building's lobby told her she had enough time to walk.

Since her arrival, snow had started falling on Manhattan in fat, lazy flakes—not enough to cause trouble, just enough to be festive. She headed south, then made the crosstown trip on East Seventy-Ninth Street to reach Central Park. Most of her walk inside the park was well within a hundred feet of Fifth Avenue, but parts of it still felt like a world away. Snow-covered branches along the rolling, tree-lined path muffled the sounds of traffic, and the subdued late morning light gave the park a soft, silvered appearance.

She passed the model-boat pond and the zoo, and emerged near the entrance to the Plaza Hotel. On Fifth Avenue, tourists and holiday shoppers swarmed the sidewalks, all collecting a dusting of snow on their hats and overcoats. Kate made her way through the crowd and the flurries until she arrived at the corner of East Fifty-Sixth, opposite the iconic, flagship store for Harry Winston, Inc.

The building had a striking main entrance: a Romanesque arch flanked by cast-iron lamps that were tall, slender, and softly glowing. A decorative iron gate spanned the arch, carved and gilded. It stood open, and led to a set of glass doors encased in steel that remained shut.

The entire façade had been decorated for the holidays—green ivy embedded with hundreds of tiny twinkling lights, like the seductive sparkle of diamonds. In case that suggestion was too subtle, a band of gem-shaped crystal lights over the arch reinforced the theme.

Waiting for the crossing signal, Kate ran her gloved fingers over the box in her pocket. For its passage through airport security, the FBI agents had provided official documents and a standard jeweler's case for the Star of the East. Once alone in her grandmother's guest bedroom, though, she had slipped the diamond back inside the Marlboro box. She couldn't explain her logic but somehow felt they should stay together.

The walk light appeared and she crossed the street. She passed between the open arms of the iron gate and through the heavy glass doors beyond it. When they closed, the clamor of New York faded, leaving her standing in the whisper-quiet foyer of the most celebrated jewelry store in the world.

Kate paused, adjusting to the sudden change in atmosphere. She looked down at a star-patterned design on the marble floor, and then up to admire a gilded bronze chandelier hanging overhead. It was when she turned her attention forward to the main salon and its even larger chandelier that she realized she was not alone, and that she was being watched.

Chapter Thirty-Four

"HOW MAY I HELP YOU?"

Spinning to face the woman who'd crisply posed the question, Kate felt a sudden heat rise up her neck.

At her insistence, and after persistent negotiations, MI6 had spent a lot of time and energy training her to be a passably capable ally for the super spy she was about to marry. Under orders from Conor's boss Frank Murdoch, a cadre of tutors coached her in the arts of "situational awareness" and "threat assessment," along with many other arcane elements of tradecraft. She felt an obligation to be worthy of their efforts, so although the lobby of a jewelry store on a busy street in broad daylight was hardly a "high-risk environment," it irked her to be caught off guard.

In her own defense, Kate thought the woman was not easily spotted, probably by design. She was to the left of the entrance, perched behind a tall, ebony credenza and in front of a mirrored wall that doubled the size of the floral displays framing her head and shoulders. This, combined with her sandy hair and earth-toned suit, made her camouflage as good as a duck blind. Clearly, the woman's job was to lie in wait and pick off the riffraff before they could breach the inner sanctum. From all appearances, she relished it. Her greeting—such as it was—was neither rude nor friendly, and her neutral expression matched its tone.

Kate walked over to the desk. The squelch of her winter boots echoed through the foyer with every step, but despite this inelegant approach she settled on an attitude of haughtiness.

"Kate Chatham, to see Phoebe Long," she said, ignoring the fact that her name would mean nothing to the store's manager because she'd never asked for it. "Could you please tell her I've arrived?"

The woman made no move to pick up the phone but gave the appointment chart in front of her a penetrating stare. "And did you book ahead?"

"Of course. We agreed to meet at noon." Kate frowned at her wristwatch while adding, "I'm sure she wrote it in her own schedule."

"I'm sure she did." With a tight-lipped smile, the woman at last reached for the phone.

A smartly dressed younger woman answered the summons and escorted Kate into the main salon. Shaped as an octagon, it had the character of a formal drawing room in an English manor house. The gilt-edged display boxes on the walls sparkled with multifaceted brilliance. All were dramatically backlit and shimmered with gem-encrusted rings, necklaces, and bracelets, as did the room's central display case.

Every corner of the room featured an elegant console table, each laid with a square of black velvet, precisely centered. At the one to the left of the entrance, a sales associate sat with a customer, murmuring over a tray of men's watches. At the far end a security guard stood in a doorway, scanning the room back to the foyer and the street beyond, but the salon was otherwise empty. The young woman invited her to sit at a table in the back corner next to the doorway, and went to find the manager.

While she waited, Kate adjusted a gilded vanity mirror on the table and studied its reflection of the room behind her. Despite the opulence, it had the sober, professional air of a savings and loan operation. Along with the guardian at the front door, this was likely meant to be intimidating. Harry Winston wanted no giggling tourists breathing over the displays and leaving fingerprints on the glass. They wanted serious customers prepared to slide over invitation-only black cards for a six-figure charge. Serious customers like her father, she thought. He had a taste for "luxury timepieces," as he called them.

A movement to her left pulled Kate's attention away from the mirrored scene to a woman who had appeared in the doorway carrying a zippered leather bag. She was attractive and tall, close to six feet in her three-inch stilettos, Kate estimated. Her medium-length blond hair was turned up in a slight flip. She looked younger than she'd sounded on the phone, but before chasing it away with a bland smile, her expression had the same harried quality Kate had noticed in her voice.

The coincidence wasn't as easy to ignore a second time. One of the world's most valuable diamonds had ended up on a dirt road in Vermont two nights ago, and here was the manager for the world's most famous jewelry house, the last known owner of that diamond, looking like she'd lost an equal number of nights' sleep.

The question Kate had posed the previous evening seemed even more relevant now. If someone had stolen the diamond from this store, why had no one reported it?

The woman greeted her as she approached, putting her smile more firmly in place. "Kate? So sorry to have kept you waiting; I'm Phoebe."

"Not at all," Kate said, shaking her hand. "I'm grateful you could fit me in on short notice."

"Of course. Let's sit down and you can tell me what brings you in today. Are we talking about something special for the holidays?"

They took their seats, facing each other across the table. Kate fingered the box in her pocket, then, trusting her instincts, she slid the diamond into her hand and rolled the Star of the East onto the square of velvet.

"Yes. We *are* talking about something special."

The strategy worked, but not quite in the way she'd expected. Its effect on Phoebe was immediate and pronounced. Her eyes grew enormous, she turned white from the base of her neck to the top of her brow, and then she fainted.

Chapter Thirty-Five

OUT COLD, Phoebe heeled to the left, toppling from her chair. Kate sprang forward, and struggled to keep the salon manager's dead weight from hitting the floor while the security guard rushed to help. Their combined efforts to get her seated again jolted her awake, but she was slow in coming to her senses. Slumped at a precarious angle, she sat blinking, her long legs splayed in boneless indifference.

Kate held Phoebe in place and brought the woman's knees together—a subtle, feminine gesture that effectively told the security guard he was out of his depth. He looked relieved to scurry off at her suggestion of a glass of water.

Glancing behind her, she saw the sales associate and his customer, both on their feet and staring at them, startled. She gave a smiling wave of reassurance.

"It's fine. She's fine," she called, and turned back to Phoebe, lowering her voice to a whisper. "We need some privacy. What's closest? Your office?"

"No. One of the VIP lounges. Around the corner."

Phoebe stared at the diamond, gleaming on its square of velvet. Kate swept it up and returned it to her pocket.

"Wait, my . . ." As though words escaped her, the salon

manager grabbled weakly at the air between her hand and the leather briefcase, just out of reach. Kate scooped that up, as well.

"Okay, let's go."

Although still dazed, Phoebe could have managed on her own, but Kate insisted on helping. She didn't understand why seeing the gem had produced such a surprising effect and seized the excuse to keep a firm grip on her.

They passed together through the central doorway, and then another on the right. The room they entered was a well-appointed lounge, with plush gray carpeting and rectangular sofas facing each other over a glass coffee table. The security guard arrived with the water and Kate took it from him with a grateful smile.

"I think we'll be okay now," she murmured, for his ears only. "It's just one of those . . . you know."

"Sure. Good." He nodded, flustered, already backing away as she shut the door.

Phoebe had dropped on to a sofa but looked more alert. Kate handed her the glass and sat down across from her. Once more, she took out the diamond and placed it on the table between them.

"I hope you won't start by pretending you don't know what it is," she said. "It will waste my time and yours."

"Of course I know what it is." Phoebe looked at her with a mixture of fear and suspicion. "But I have no idea who *you* are. Or why you have it."

Kate had expected the question, but not in this context. Her original strategy had been to walk into the store, tell the entertaining tale about the deer and what followed, and see what information she could gather about the diamond's current owner. She hadn't planned on coming face-to-face with a rattled . . . what? Witness? Accomplice?

FBI agents Knox and Toomey had not expected it, either, or they would never have allowed her to be here alone, but it was too late to do anything about that now.

She sifted through the details Conor had provided during their phone calls and decided to again rely on a hunch, beginning with the man who started the entire chain of events right here in New York. She pulled the Marlboro box from her pocket and dropped it next to the diamond.

"Suppose I told you Cyril sent me."

"Oh, dear God." Phoebe looked terrified. The color just returning to her face began shifting toward green.

Satisfied she'd hit the target, but alarmed it might lead to something more disruptive than fainting, Kate tried to stifle Phoebe's reaction.

"Listen, he didn't, okay? Cyril didn't send me, but I know who he is." *Barely*, Kate's inner voice added. "I can see you're afraid, but you need to tell me what's been happening here."

"Are you from the police?" Phoebe looked as though she hoped for an affirmative reply.

She shook her head. "I'm not, but I'm help— working with them."

"Working with them? What does that mean? What are you?"

Sensing her advantage slipping away, Kate groped and pulled something from memory.

"Special Operations."

WHAT are you doing? The inner voice was hissing now, but she ignored it.

Maybe it sounded convincing, or maybe Phoebe just wanted to believe it, grasping at any opportunity to tell her story to someone who might help her. Whichever the case, she accepted the answer and looked at her, expectant and attentive.

Kate pointed at the diamond. "Let's start with this. Can you tell me who the current owner is?"

Phoebe answered without hesitating, an eager student tackling a flash card quiz.

"The Arab Republic of Egypt."

The unexpected name—of a government, no less—rocked her, but then Kate saw the obvious connection, remembering Conor's description of Cyril.

A Coptic Christian who moved to New York from Alexandria.

The man Lucie and Jimmy met in New York, and who hid the Star of the East in the truck they drove back to Canada, was Egyptian. The man he was sending it to—Captain Mounir—had a Coptic cross tattoo on his wrist, so the odds were good he was Egyptian, too.

If Jimmy hadn't ruined their plans, first by putting it in his pocket and next by panicking and sticking it inside a deer, the diamond would be on board Mounir's ship by now, en route to the Arab Republic of Egypt.

"Go on," Kate said, recovering her wits.

Phoebe looked uncertain. "I'm not sure where to start. How much do you already know?"

"For the sake of simplicity, let's assume it's nothing."

Nodding, Phoebe sat back on the couch, and after a long draw from the water glass, she began talking.

Chapter Thirty-Six

CONSIDERING HOW IT BEGAN, Kate thought she should have realized when she got out of bed that she would spend the rest of the day behind schedule. Since leaving the Harry Winston salon, the last several hours had been a blur of stop-and-go movement—of cabs and phone calls and voice messages, of waiting impatiently, only to race forward and wait again.

She'd tried to reach Conor in multiple ways, starting with repeated attempts to the number he'd used when calling her—Reid's cell phone. Either the battery was dead or it was far from any waiting hand, because no one ever answered it.

After some searching, she found the main number for the hospital in La Malbaie, but got nowhere of course, because patient information was confidential and they could tell her nothing of Reid Briggs or any of his companions. She couldn't remember the name of the hotel he'd mentioned. More research revealed it as Le Manoir Richelieu, but she struck out there, also. The receptionist transferred her to his room, and the line rang out with no answer.

At last, she called the inn, hoping to get Dominic, but the run of bad luck continued when Abigail picked up instead.

"Have you heard from Conor at all?" Kate asked, after getting through the opening pleasantries.

"Have *I* heard from him?" Abigail said. "Why the hell would I? Isn't he there with you?"

Kate gritted her teeth. There had been no time to bring Abigail up to speed on all the details of last night's events, nor was there any now. She finessed the question by firing back her own request.

"Not at the moment, so if he happens to call, can you or Dominic just ask him to phone my cell?"

"What's going on?" Abigail demanded, as always, refusing to be finessed.

Kate wished she hadn't tried the inn at all, now. "I'll explain everything later. Just tell him to call me, if you hear from him."

At last, she turned her attention to addressing what she most dreaded—three missed calls and two voicemails from her grandmother. Without bothering to play the messages, she phoned the apartment, squeezing her eyes shut while it rang, bracing herself when Sophia came on the line.

"Where on earth are you, Kate?" she demanded, sounding mildly exasperated. "I thought you would be back by now. It's almost four thirty. Did you forget we're having an early dinner before the party? Jeannette and Richard are here already."

"I'm so sorry, Oma. Something came up and I—"

Sophia sailed on, talking over her as if she hadn't spoken. "And Conor has been here for nearly two hours. I had to tell him—"

"Wait, what? Conor is there? Right now? At your apartment?"

"Yes, of course at my apartment. I told him I couldn't reach you, so now you've worried him. Honestly Kate," she scolded, "I promised I would keep trying if he would take a nap. He looks like he was up all night. He's been in Canada since yesterday, he said? You didn't mention that. And there are stitches in his chin. Work related, he said. I don't understand what sort of work this is, that ends up with stitches in the chin. And is he growing a beard, Kate? He won't have it for the wedding, I hope? I don't like it at all."

"He didn't have it when he left yesterday." Kate tried to process the fire hose of news while dodging groups of people who were clearly not on a tight schedule. "Maybe he just hasn't shaved today. It grows fast."

"It makes him look shifty, and he's too handsome for a beard."

"Agreed on both counts. Oma, I need to talk to him. Wake him up and put him on the phone."

She listened as her grandmother carried the cordless receiver through the penthouse, hearing an echo of voices, followed by Sophia's firm step on the marble floor of the entrance hall. There was a period of silence before a muffled exchange, and at last, there it was, the sleepy, husky voice that melted her every single time she heard it.

"Thanks for bringing the tux. I was betting you'd shredded it."

"Conor, I don't—how are you even there? What happened? How did you get to New York so fast?"

"On a Learjet air ambulance, supplied by our friends in London. Reid needs emergency surgery. He wanted his own man at Mt. Sinai doing the job. The funny bit is I thought I'd be going to Frank on bended knee, but it turns out I had the golden key to an Egyptian army plot MI6 has been foostering over for ages."

Conor sounded animated and chatty now, which was par for the course. He had a habit of popping awake and alert in an instant while she was struggling to open her eyes.

"I'll tell you about it later. Where are *you* by the way? Not still at Harry Winston's, surely? Your sister's raging, and your grandmother wants to light the candles on a Christmas tree in the library, which is a bloody terrifying tradition, if I'm being honest. How has she not burnt the building down in all these years?"

"I'm not sure," Kate said, only half listening. She scanned the scribbled notes in her hand and turned in a slow circle, trying get her bearings. "Conor, tell me about this Egyptian army thing."

Something in her voice must have gotten through. When Conor spoke next, the lilting playfulness had disappeared.

"Kate, where are you?"

She closed her eyes again and took a deep breath. "I just landed at Dorval Airport in Montreal."

Chapter Thirty-Seven

"YOU ARE AT DORVAL AIRPORT. In Montreal."

It wasn't a question, nor was it the incredulous yelp of a man left alone with his fiancée's relatives. Conor had simply repeated her news with quiet precision. After a pause long enough for a sharp intake of breath, his follow-up was just as measured.

"Alone, or is someone with you?"

From another man, the question and the eerie calm of its delivery might have sounded loaded and laced with suspicion. Coming from the one she loved and knew so well, it flooded Kate with relief, because it signaled they were on the same page. He had no idea what was going on, but Conor's operational radar had already engaged.

Translated, his question meant: *Do you have backup with you for whatever the hell you are doing in Montreal?*

She wished she had a better answer for both of them.

"It looks like I'm on my own. I called the FBI, but I didn't connect with Agent Toomey until a few minutes ago. He said it would take hours to work out the jurisdiction issues, and by then it'll be too late."

"What do you need? I'll ask Nicky to get the RCMP over to you."

"You could try, I suppose, but I think the issues would be the same for them."

A whispered obscenity hissed down the line.

"Right. Let's hear the rest of it, so."

"There's not a lot of time," she warned.

"Then talk fast, Kate," Conor shot back, giving her a glimpse of the state of his nerves.

"Okay. Yes, okay."

Between the notes she'd written and the airport's signage, Kate had oriented herself and saw the landmark she was looking for—a restaurant a few hundred feet past the duty-free shop. Feeling less frantic now, she walked to an empty departure gate. She chose a corner and sat facing the window, away from the aimless movements of Saturday travelers and the zippering pitch of luggage wheels.

"I've got about forty minutes, and you have to go first this time, Conor. Tell me how the diamond connects to Frank's Egyptian army plot. My side of this can wait."

She could hear him gathering wind to blast away her opinion of who should go first, but after a groaning sigh he surprised her.

"Fair enough. You're right."

Whatever he was feeling, Conor bottled it up and delivered the brief she needed. It startled her when he began with the Egyptian president, Hosni Mubarak.

"He's twenty years in power now and after becoming a proper tyrant," he said. "Corruption, illegal detentions, rumors of torture—you can tick all the boxes. There's lakes of Egyptians thinking it's time the guy fecked off, and everyone's intelligence says the place is a powder keg waiting for a match. Some want a repeat of the first revolution, when the army took down King Farouk, but Mubarak has been bribing his generals for a long time with high salaries and fancy houses, so they can't be arsed with a coup."

Conor paused the rapid-fire narrative. "How's it going down, then—still with me?"

"Still here," Kate said. She stared at the runway, where an Air

Canada plane had launched a curling wave of snow with its rumbling progress. "So, if the generals are fat and happy, where's the plot?"

"I'm coming to that bit next," he said. "I told Frank about this Coptic cross symbol showing up everywhere, and it sounded familiar to him. He made a few calls and was fairly excited when he rang me back. MI6 and the CIA have been grabbing intercepts between an Egyptian Lieutenant-General and a US-based contact they hadn't identified yet. Both are Coptic, and the intercepts show they're part of a network that's organizing for a people's revolution to get rid of Mubarak."

Frank had explained that Coptic Christians were perennial victims of violence and repression in Egypt, but their current pope was one of Mubarak's most vocal cheerleaders. With rumors of the pope getting paid for his support, many in the community feared the repercussions of a popular revolt.

"If they're seen as collaborators with Mubarak because of their pope," Conor said, "the Copts will have even bigger targets on their backs. So, a group of them linked up with the diaspora in the US to raise money and shower it on high-ranking Egyptian generals. The idea is to persuade the army to support a popular revolt, and to protect the Coptic community from any fallout."

"Frank thinks Cyril is part of this group?" Kate asked, anxious to move the story along, hoping something in it would help her decide what to do. "They're using the Star of the East to bribe a general?"

"Probably not with the diamond, but with the millions they'd get from selling it. Frank seems dead certain, and I've connected him with Nicky to follow up on it. This operation has the marks of others they uncovered after the fact. Mounir was bringing the Star of the East to Alexandria on his ship, but the Hollumborg got rerouted and won't reach Egypt for another two weeks. Cyril must be on a deadline with his buyer, because he was sending a courier to get the diamond back from Mounir at the ship's next port of call, which—"

The midsentence break was so abrupt Kate might have assumed the connection had dropped. While telling a story, Conor was like a boat in full sail, impossible to bring to a stop. She knew he was still there, though, and what had brought him up short. His narrative had caught up with hers.

She looked down at the airport's tarmac—a busy little city, with service trucks chugging over floodlit routes—and picked up the tale herself, beginning with the line he hadn't finished.

"Which is Montreal. The courier was scheduled to be at the Hotel Bonaventure's bar in Montreal at three o'clock today, but never showed up."

"Bloody hell." Conor sounded both excited and alarmed. "You know who the courier is."

"I know who it was supposed to be," Kate said. "I'm the courier now."

Chapter Thirty-Eight

WHEN PHOEBE HAD SHARED her story in the salon's VIP room, she began in a manner that reminded Kate of a children's fairy tale about treasure locked in rooms within rooms. Harry Winston kept its rarest and most valuable jewels in a double-locked area, inside the main vault, with each gem in its own locker.

"Like a safe deposit locker, but, well, more upscale," Phoebe said. "Only the salon manager has access, and the key to only one of the two that open each locker."

"Who keeps the other keys?" Kate asked.

"It depends on the stone, but most are held by Buying and Sourcing, in a separate building down the street. On Wednesday, I got a call from Becca, a manager in that department. She told me to get here early on Thursday to meet the Egyptian Consulate's head of security. He was bringing the key for number eighteen and would take the stone away with him."

Kate picked up the diamond again to hold in her palm, running a thumb over its cool surface. It had been mined from the earth, so the term "stone" was appropriate but somehow inadequate.

"Did you know what the . . . stone was, in number eighteen?"

"Yes," Phoebe said. "Sometimes, Becca or someone else from

the executive suite comes over to host a viewing for VIPs and they'll tell me which keys to have ready. Once, when the event was over, Becca swore me to secrecy and showed me the Star of the East. She said the Egyptian government bought it from Harry Winston just before he died but left it in our vault, and it had been in number eighteen ever since."

"Did Becca say why they wanted to take it now?"

"She didn't know. We both laughed a little about how it was like losing a friend." Phoebe gave a tremulous smile then continued with forced strength, as if wanting to expel the story and shed its burden.

"So, on Thursday morning, a man named Cyril arrived with two men—Consulate security staff, he said. He showed his ID and the key, and he gave me a copy of the paperwork that came from Buying and Sourcing. I brought him to the vault and we finished everything in ten minutes. Before he left, I mentioned our courier service, saying we'd be happy to see the Star of the East safely back to Egypt if needed."

"What does the service involve?" Kate asked.

"For a diamond of this value, someone would hand-carry it in a locked case, get it through TSA screening, customs, all of that. Anyway, he said he didn't need a courier, and I wish I hadn't said anything because that's where everything went wrong, but I didn't know it then."

Kate leaned forward. "How so?"

Phoebe took another gulp of water. "Yesterday, the receptionist called to say someone had asked to see me in my office."

The visitor turned out to be one of the men Cyril had described as security staff the day before. He said the diplomatic staff member charged with transporting the Star of the East had been delayed by meetings in Montreal. They needed someone to pick up the diamond at his hotel and facilitate it through the airport's international zone. There, she would rendezvous with another diplomatic officer who was flying in from Cairo to pick it up from her.

"Which all sounded fine," Phoebe said. "But then he insisted the courier needed to be there on Saturday—well, today, in fact—and that it had to be me!"

She raised her hands in a limp gesture of disbelief. For the first time, some color came into her face and a little spirit into her voice.

Kate knew nothing about the hierarchy of positions within the jewel industry, but Phoebe's attitude suggested the one called "courier" must be near the bottom. The salon manager found the man's proposal absurd and insulting. She tried to assure him they had capable, more appropriate staff to provide this service but he ignored her protests, and made no effort to be subtle in his persuasion.

"First, he said this was a matter of national importance to the Egyptian government, and then, he *literally* said, 'You have no choice.' He named a corporate director on the Harry Winston Board and said he was a friend of the Consul General. He was threatening to get me fired. At the time it all seemed ridiculous, but I didn't want to alienate the Consulate. I thought I could sort everything out with Becca. She's dating one of the corporate directors. So, I told him I'd start making the arrangements, but he said they'd taken care of that."

Phoebe stopped and again turned pale, as if just remembering how the story ended.

"He handed me one of those flat express mail boxes and said my discretion would be—how did he put it? Richly, or handsomely compensated, something flowery like that. Then, he thanked me and left."

She began trembling as her eyes filled. "I had no reason to question any of this. Everyone had ID, Cyril had the right key, and the paperwork from Buying and Sourcing was all in order. The car they parked in front of the building had diplomatic plates. I never suspected a thing until I opened the box."

Afraid she might faint again Kate hurried to sit next to her, soothing and bracing her with a supporting arm.

"It's okay, and you're okay. You've done nothing wrong. What was in the box? Where did you—oh. It's in this, isn't it?"

At Phoebe's mute nod, she reached for the large leather bag at her feet. Placing it on the coffee table, she unzipped the top, and looking inside, saw why the salon manager was so badly frightened.

Chapter Thirty-Nine

"CASH," Conor said. He was guessing, and Kate rolled her eyes because, of course, he'd nailed it.

"So much for that big reveal."

"Don't blame me, you're the one who needs to hurry."

She smiled at this flicker of humor and glanced at her watch. She had enough time but thought she might need to move before long. The departure gate was coming to life around her. A flight announcement had appeared on the digital board behind the check-in station and travelers were filing in, trailing their carry-ons.

"You are correct, Sherlock. Cash. Lots and lots of it. Wrapped like those bricks you see people in mafia films throwing into gym bags."

Conor gave a low whistle. "I guess you could call that 'handsomely compensated,' and, I suppose, compromising."

"I had the same thought," Kate agreed. "It seems as if they wanted Phoebe to look complicit, but I didn't tell her that."

Along with the cash, the box contained a small jeweler's case and three boarding passes—one was for a flight from LaGuardia to Montreal at 12:35. There was another for a Frankfurt flight, leaving at 6:45, which was simply to allow her to access the international boarding zone. The third was for her return flight to New York, leaving at 6:35.

"The boarding passes freaked her out more than the money," Kate said. "They would have needed all her personal information to book those flights. And then, of course, there was a typed list of instructions that didn't look anything like the typical gig for a Harry Winston courier."

"What did she do?" Conor asked.

"First, she tried to get in touch with her colleague at Buying and Sourcing, Becca, but the staff there said she'd already left for the weekend. So, her next move was to call the Egyptian Consulate."

"And they had nobody there named Cyril." He was skipping ahead again, but wide of the mark this time. She felt gratified to keep at least one surprise intact.

"Wrong. Although, he wasn't the head of security, because they have a private contractor for that, but they did have a nondiplomatic member of the staff named Cyril. He's employed as the Consul General's personal driver. That explains how he had a consular ID and a car with diplomatic plates."

Conor hummed in appreciation. "Impressive infiltration."

"Not necessarily, but I'll get to that in a minute."

The departure gate was filling up now, and there were too many bored-looking occupants sitting too close, with nothing better to do than listen to a stranger's conversation. It's what she'd be doing, after all.

With the phone to her ear, Kate slipped away to stake out a new position along the concourse. Between the incessant chimes of the public address system, and the bilingual appeals for missing passengers to proceed immediately to where they should already be, there was little chance of anyone hearing her.

She chose a spot across from the restrooms and continued, describing Phoebe's paralyzed state of mind when Kate had arrived at noon. The salon manager now realized she had handed over a world-famous gem to someone who'd lied about who he was and might not be acting for the Egyptian government at all. On the other hand, if it was legitimate, she'd just botched the most important customer service assignment of her life, and calling the police would make it monumentally worse. Seeing no good options, Phoebe had done nothing.

"She was already terrified at what Cyril might do once he found out she hadn't shown up. When I arrived and rolled the diamond out in front of her she fainted."

"Uh-huh," Conor grunted. "Sure with the nerves scalded off her she'd have to, wouldn't she? What a piece of luck you arrived in time to take the second half of her assignment."

His air of nonchalance wasn't convincing, and she suspected he didn't intend it to be.

"Um, yes, she was pretty relieved."

"I can well imagine," Conor said. "What I'm struggling to understand is why you've done it, Kate. You're in Montreal to meet someone who expects you to hand over a diamond that's been stolen from the government of Egypt by Cyril the chauffeur. You're not seriously going through with this?"

"I don't know what I'm going to do," Kate said. "I'm hoping things will come clear once the contact shows up."

"What possible difference does it make who the contact is?"

"Quite a lot, actually. The instructions say it's going to be Cyril's boss, the Consul General."

"Oh for—"

Kate pushed on, interrupting the burst of profanity. "I found a picture of him online, so I'll recognize him. If it *is* him, it means there's still a chance this diamond might not be stolen at all, but after what you've just told me about this Coptic group, it's also possible one of the top diplomatic representatives for the Egyptian government is part of a plot to bribe its generals and overthrow his own president."

"Bloody hell," Conor muttered. "How did we ever get from

date night to this feckin' bag of snakes?" He released a tight sigh of frustration. "Fine. Let's get on to this list of instructions, which are apparently now *your* instructions. Crack on, so."

Chapter Forty

REGISTERING CONOR'S TENSION, Kate tried to sound cool and unconcerned as she explained Phoebe's instructions, in which the famous Marlboro box had a starring role.

From Lucie Vallencourt's story, they knew Cyril had placed the diamond in the cigarette box and taped it inside the truck she drove back to Canada. Kate estimated he'd done it soon after taking it from the Harry Winston salon Thursday morning, because Lucie and Jimmy came for the truck early that afternoon.

"If everything had gone according to plan, Mounir would have found the diamond last night. Cyril must have told him to use the box as a signal, because Phoebe's instructions say when she got to the hotel bar she should look for a Marlboro box with the symbol of a cross on it."

Kate explained Phoebe was told to transfer the diamond to the jeweler's case and return to Dorval. At five o'clock she would sit at a bar called Skyscapes with the empty cigarette box and jeweler's case on the counter next to her, and wait for the contact.

"Since Jimmy sent Cyril's plan off the rails, I've already got the Marlboro box and the diamond, and Phoebe had the case," Kate said. "I was able to book a 2:20 flight to Montreal, and I just duplicated the other two tickets. We didn't cancel hers in case it triggered an email to whoever booked them."

"And, of course, you had your passport with you," Conor said.

"You told me to always carry it with me, just in—"

"Just in case. I know. I remember. What you don't have is back up, and you're within ten minutes of contact. It's hours since Mounir should have confirmed the transfer. Nobody knows he's sitting in a Canadian jail, but by now they must assume something's gone arseways. They need to play it through, but will be on guard and prepared for trouble.

"Maybe it *will* be the Consul General," Conor went on, firing off his assessment as though talking to himself. "Or maybe it will be some Coptic insurrectionist, and yes, I suppose the two aren't mutually exclusive. Whoever it is, I'm betting Cyril gave them a description of Phoebe. Do you share any physical resemblance with her, whatsoever?"

"She's blond and about four inches taller than me," Kate admitted.

"Fantastic. So, you'll be a sitting duck at the Skyscapes bar, with your cigarette box and jeweler's case. What, *exactly*, was your plan?"

The question was fair, but his caustic delivery strained Kate's patience.

"I didn't *exactly* have one," she snapped. "I couldn't get through to the FBI agents because they were too busy getting their jewel thief back to prison, and since you left your 'bloody' cell phone sitting on the kitchen counter I had to call every other number I could think of but couldn't find you, either. Phoebe was a basket case, so not an option. I get it, I'm not the perfect stand-in, but I figured it was better to keep all the options open and hope for the best. Therefore, here I am, making it up as I go along, and to be honest this conversation didn't help much. I still don't know what to do, but now I know the stakes are a lot higher than I thought, so thanks for that."

She rested her head against the wall of the concourse and

closed her eyes.

"Kate? Are you there? Don't hang up." Conor sounded alarmed.

"I didn't." She opened her eyes, refreshed from the release of temper. "But, I'll need to pretty soon if I'm going through with this. If I do, whoever shows up will take the Star of the East and maybe use it to bring down the Egyptian president. If I bring it home right now we may never find out who was behind all this, or we might discover it was the government after all, and we'll have triggered a diplomatic incident for keeping their diamond when they wanted it back."

Having bluntly identified the stakes, she thought the answer was obvious, but she asked, anyway. "What do you think Frank would want me to do?"

She heard a hint of weary laughter in Conor's response.

"Do we really want to be going down that aul' road? I've never found it too healthy, doing what Frank wanted."

"Well, then," Kate said quietly, "what would you have done differently? What would you do now, if you were here instead of me?"

She waited, listening to Conor's breathing, and the whispery static of air passing over his mouthpiece, which told her he was pacing the room.

"I'd have done nothing differently," he said, at last. "My instincts would have been the same. You've got to play it through, as well. Make choices that keep the most options open. Hope they're the right ones."

There was something in his flat admission that sounded deflated, as if acknowledging defeat.

"I guess we can call this my first solo mission," she said, trying to lighten the mood. "It might be worse. I'm not on some dark, lonesome road. This terminal is mobbed, so how dangerous can it be?"

"Well, it's double what it would have been, now you've jinxed it," Conor said.

As a jest, it was a weak attempt. Over the line and across the miles she felt his anxiety for her. She was surprised to be free of any herself but had begun questioning the wisdom of her decisions. She'd made them quickly, but not in the emotional, impulsive style that had always been her trademark.

She followed instincts that felt natural and right and entirely new, and Conor had admitted they agreed with his, but Kate knew she would never match his broader talents and skills. That didn't bother her; but the idea that her own talents might be inadequate for the job at hand . . . that did.

She wondered if Conor's silence meant his thoughts were following a similar track, but when he spoke again she realized he'd been on a completely different one.

"It's a test for us both," he said. "And if you were anywhere my two feet could reach in the next ten minutes, I'm sure I'd fail it. I'd come rocketing in, take it all away from you, and give myself a bollocking, later. You need a partner, not a bodyguard. I'm not there yet, but that shouldn't be your problem." Conor cleared the gravel-edged hoarseness in his voice. "You're trained and well able for it, Kate. This one's all yours."

The words were important, but the confidence she heard in them—unforced and sincere—was everything. She could only imagine how deep he had reached for this conviction, and the means to express it, but he'd managed both.

Stunned, Kate straightened from her slouch against the terminal's wall, trying to find words to accept a gift she hadn't expected, but that had arrived exactly on time.

"I'll make it count. I promise," she said, then rolled her eyes at her own cliché. Conor answered with a wry laugh.

"Settle yourself, Danger Girl. Just make your flight back to New York. I'll be waiting, sweating out a tux at the Pierre Hotel. About that, by the way. What, for the love of Jesus and Mary, am I to be telling your gran—and the rest of your family—about any of this?"

Kate smiled. "I was awake most of last night wondering that myself. I hadn't worked it out yet, but good luck with it."

Chapter Forty-One

CONOR STOOD at the bedroom window, still gripping the phone, estimating the level of pressure required to shatter it, wondering if he should test the theory.

Across the East River, he could just make out the shadowed outline of a stone pillar—the Roosevelt Island Lighthouse. It looked lonely on its desolate sliver of land. The wan glow of its lamp had little chance against the murky December night, but the light held steady regardless, illuminating itself, if nothing else.

"And the darkness comprehended it not."

He recited the biblical verse without conscious thought, then blinked and scowled at his reflection in the glass.

"Where the hell did that come from? Get a bleedin' grip, McBride."

With some effort, he put the phone down, resting it on the window ledge, allowing the rigid talons at the end of his arm to resume the natural shape of a hand.

It was six minutes past five o'clock, six minutes past the appointed hour for Kate's Skyscapes rendezvous at Dorval Airport. Before signing off, she'd promised to call after the meeting ended. Had the contact not shown yet? Were they having a friendly chat?

Maybe the battery in her mobile had died. Or, maybe the timeline that defined "after" for Kate was simply more elastic than his own.

For the moment, these were the options Conor allowed himself. He wasn't sure how long it would take for others to breach his mental barricade but he could hold out for at least an hour. He owed her that much, and he had a few other things to tackle in the meantime.

Turning from the window, he rubbed a few fingers over his chin, surprised again when they met a crosshatched inch of stitches. He needed a shower and a shave, but most of all he needed a story, and the two knocks that came now—quiet, but firm—told him he'd run out of time for constructing one.

He opened the door to Sophia, already dressed for the evening in a sapphire blue gown. High-necked and long-sleeved, it flattered her slender figure. With a diamond brooch pinned in the gathered material at her waist, she looked exquisite and formidably regal as she stood in the doorway, arms crossed.

"And?" she demanded. "Dinner is in half an hour, whether she's here or not. What's happened, for heaven's sake? This rudeness isn't like Kate at all."

"It's not. At all. I'm sorry, Sophia, and so is Kate, but something's come up."

"Yes, yes, 'something's come up,'" she said, rejecting his insipid preamble. "Kate said as much, and now you've repeated it, but this tells me nothing."

"I know." He opened the door wider. "Do you want to come in, and I can try to explain it?"

"No. I'd like you to wash, shave, and put on your evening clothes."

"Right so. I will. I'll do it now."

"And come to the library when you're finished."

"I'll be there in twenty minutes."

"Make it fifteen."

"Fifteen minutes. Right."

Closing the door, Conor rested his forehead against it and

swore softly. Most of Kate's family could feck off into the sea, for all he cared, but Sophia was different. The warmth and beauty and feistiness he loved in Kate were all visible in her grandmother, in her smile and the sparkle of her eyes. From the moment they'd met and bonded over a Schumann lullaby, she had been his best ally. He valued her good opinion of him, and her friendship, and knew he was in danger now of losing both. She was smart enough to see straight through any slippery tale of half-truths, and if he insisted on trying to sell one, she might never forgive him.

He obeyed the royal summons and presented himself fifteen minutes later with his hair still wet but neatly combed, and every crease and button of his tux in its proper place.

When Conor had first visited Sophia's penthouse earlier in the year, he'd been surprised by its comfortable atmosphere, and the library was by far his favorite space. It had everything anyone could ask for in a room—a fireplace, comfortable chairs, walls full of books and oil paintings, an apartment-sized baby grand piano, and a large drinks cabinet in the corner. This evening, it also had a Fraser fir Christmas tree in another corner. Now ablaze with lit candles, it looked every bit as alarming as he'd expected.

Kate's sister Jeannette and her husband, Richard, wineglasses in hand, were admiring it with Sophia when he entered, but clearly there had been a prearranged signal for their exit. As soon as Conor appeared, Jeannette put a glass of white wine in his hand, then she and Richard made their excuses and disappeared to the more formal living room downstairs.

Conor put the glass on a coffee table stacked with catalogues from the Museum of Modern Art, and took up a standing position in front of the princess's wingback chair.

"Kate's in Montreal," he said, without preamble. "I know that sounds mad—well, it is mad, right enough—but it's the solid truth, and it's about all the truth I can give you at the minute, except that she'll be late for the party, if she makes it at all."

Not taking her eyes from him, Sophia placed her glass of wine on the table as well.

"Is she safe?"

Conor hesitated, not only to form a careful response but because the question, combined with a certain sharp awareness in Sophia's eyes, startled him.

"I'm sure she is. I've no reason to think otherwise," he said.

"Is this something she's doing for you?"

He took even longer to answer this one. Conor looked at the beautifully decorated tree, watching a dozen small flames dance within inches of its branches, and then studied her thoughtfully. She met his gaze with the barest hint of a smile. He read it as an invitation to confess but parried her question with his own.

"Why would you ask me that?"

"Well, you've been in Canada, you told me. Work related."

Conor had to smile himself, now, enjoying the chess match he knew she was going to win.

"I did say that, and it's the only truth I can tell about that as well, but I'm getting the idea you've drawn your own conclusions, anyway."

"Are they the right ones?"

"Depends what you're basing them on."

"Sit down, Conor." Sophia tapped the arm of the sofa next to her chair. He did as she asked without another word, bringing the wineglass with him.

"Last year, on the day of my eightieth birthday, someone shot you in the chest, on a golf course, in the dark. Kate informed me an illegal hunter had mistaken you for a deer."

After throwing back half the wine in his glass, Conor surrendered with a sheepish grin.

"Cracking story, wasn't it?"

"Not so much cracking as patently ridiculous."

"Sure I thought the same when she told me, the day I got out of hospital. In fairness, though, you're the only member of the bloody family who doesn't believe it. The rest are still slagging me over it."

He was laughing now, but stopped at Sophia's expression. It was sad, disappointed.

"I've been waiting ever since for the real story, wondering why neither of you could share it with me, and whether you both thought me such an old fool as that."

"Well, that's only pure rubbish."

Conor took her hand. He'd never dared such a gesture before, not that he didn't feel the affection it implied. Despite her easy warmth and good nature, Sophia was every inch a royal princess, and he was an Irishman still fresh from the boat, naturally allergic to aristocracy, ignorant of its protocols. He was afraid to make a mistake with her, but feeling a squeeze from her fingers, he relaxed.

"Foolish is the last thing—the dead last thing—either of us would ever think about you," he said. "Don't blame Kate for any of this. It's my fault, entirely. This has been hard on her, hiding things from you, but I'm ashamed I never realized how it would affect you. I apologize, Sophia. I can only say my instincts were protective."

"Overprotective, perhaps. According to what I've heard, at least."

He winced, looking down at the library's plush, leaf-patterned carpet. "Overprotective," he agreed. "But, not always irrationally so. I think she'd have to admit that."

"She has," Sophia said. The pressure of her hand added weight to the reassurance. "But, in a manner so vague I find it maddening. I want something better from my granddaughter, and from the man who wants to marry her. In fact, I demand it."

Alarmed, Conor searched her face, looking for evidence of the threat her words suggested, but there wasn't any. He saw only a radiant smile, an echo of the one that had knocked him sideways the first time he'd seen it.

"Don't look so afraid, Conor. You may shock me, but I very much doubt it will change anything. I made up my mind about you ages ago, and it had nothing to do with Schumann."

Modulating an explosive sigh, he nodded. "I'll tell you everything about myself. I'd start spilling it all this minute, but it would take the rest of the night. What happened last year is something different, and it's not for me to share that story. You'll need to get it from Kate, and I need to warn you, it'll be painful for her to talk about, and for you to hear.

"As for what's going on right now . . . I can sketch the outline for you, if you'll trust me to make it more sensible later."

Sophia arranged herself in her chair, preparing to listen. "I will trust you, as long as it's not some fanciful story about a deer."

She looked startled by his burst of laughter, which only made it harder for Conor to stop.

Chapter Forty-Two

ON CLOSER INSPECTION, Skyscapes looked less like a restaurant and more like a nightclub where daylight hours did not exist. On the surrounding walls, an electric color glowed through milky glazed panels, supplying light at its barest minimum. At the front, the bar ran down the edge of the concourse. Encased in the same translucent material, it had a ghostly, holographic quality. As Kate approached, it was bathed in neon pink; by the time she'd taken a seat, the color had changed to purple.

A sprinkling of customers sat along its length with their backs to the terminal, facing the moody ambience of the interior. The only concession made to the time of day was the choice of music. Instead of a throbbing house beat, a gelatinous French version of "White Christmas" poured from the speakers.

Kate ordered a sparkling water and paid for it, then began arranging her tokens next to her—cigarette box, jeweler's case, and a current issue of *The New Yorker* magazine.

The wallet-sized case had a spongy layer of butterscotch leather covering a hard shell. As instructed, she spun the combination dials to lock it before placing it on the bar, then patted her head to see how her attempted disguise was holding up.

If challenged, she'd invented a backup story with Phoebe's

help, but had still done her best to maximize her resemblance to the salon manager. Before grabbing a cab to LaGuardia, she dashed two blocks up Fifth Avenue to Bergdorf Goodman. Snatching up the largest winter hat she could find—a knitted version of the newsboy style, black, with a faux fur pompom—she tucked every last strand of auburn hair into it. It wasn't perfect, but it would have to do.

There was no time for any schemes to look four inches taller, but since she was already sitting at the bar, the difference in height wouldn't be noticeable, unless someone observed her approach.

Betraying no particular interest, she took in the faces around her in casual, fleeting glances and saw a diverse gathering. Some were well dressed, others in sweatpants. Few looked either more or less like diplomatic staff; any or all of them could be criminals.

At one end of the bar, four young women with backpacks were in a hilarious mood. The eruptions of loud laughter, combined with their flushed, animated faces, implied happy hour had started long ago, perhaps as early as lunchtime. Had she really been Frankfurt-bound, Kate was 100 percent certain the backpackers would have been on her flight, and in her row.

As the last minutes ticked away, she sipped her water and considered the remaining decisions she had to make.

Play it through.

While speaking with Conor, she had been considering the action implied in those words, but chose not to draw his attention to it.

With incremental steps, including a big one today, he'd expanded his tolerance for risk where it involved her. Given they'd been at the bubble-wrap level only months ago, the progress was exponential. It felt unfair to test his stamina by sharing her operational ideas for gaining the initiative, but she'd been sliding them around in her own mind.

She had already gone off script in one respect. Kate was still considering its impact on other options when all of them suddenly shrank to zero.

With all her identifying objects on the bar to her right, her peripheral gaze was focused in that direction, but the presence she felt now surged in from the left and moved quickly behind her. Whoever it was, he had his own ideas about gaining the initiative, making contact in the most literal sense. A rush of adrenaline doubled her heart rate as two hands gripped her upper arms. Then, through a wiry scratch of beard, his lips—flaccid and ice-cold—pressed a kiss onto the back of her neck.

"Ah, my love. Have you waited very long? I'm sorry."

The greeting wasn't meant for her ears alone. His musical, sibilant voice sounded cheerful, but when she instinctively pulled away his grip tightened. When he bent forward a second time, the words were only for her, and they weren't friendly.

"Listen to me. No, don't move yet. If you are quiet and calm and do what I say, things will be fine. Do you understand?"

"Yes."

"Mmm. Good."

Again, his beard nuzzled at her neck. Kate stiffened, hands balled in her lap, willing herself to keep still.

"You are delighted to see me. You are going to collect these items on the bar, and we will leave together, arm in arm. If you cry out or resist, things will go badly for you. This, also, you perfectly understand?"

"Yes." Her initial shock was subsiding, allowing space for a growing anger, but Kate kept her voice low and frightened. "I don't know what this is about, but I followed all the instructions. Take the case and let me go."

"*All* of the instructions?"

He chuckled, then, straightening, he yanked off her hat and tossed it onto the bar before resuming his grip on her arm.

"You've colored your hair, my darling. Is it that, or something else? You look like a different person."

If she'd had any doubts remaining, this final, loaded observation would have ended them. The man exhibited neither the professionalism nor the cultured style of a career diplomat, and he most certainly was not the Consul General, whose recent photo online showed him as clean-shaven.

Drawing on every bit of training she could remember, she steadied herself, determined to play it through.

She half turned, not trying yet to see the bearded stranger behind her. He wouldn't look familiar, but she didn't need to recognize the face to know him. Kate assumed her role as commanded, allowing her gaze to wander to one side while offering a vague, bored smile.

"Well, red is my color. I hope you like it, Cyril."

Chapter Forty-Three

FROM THE WAY his grip loosened, Kate could tell he hadn't expected her to address him by name. He covered his surprise with another offensive gesture of intimacy, bending to caress her ear, but this time she was ready. Careful to make the movement appear natural, she dropped her head back, slamming it against his mouth, and heard the satisfying crack of his teeth knocking together. Tugging him down by the lapel of his coat she spoke with the same suggestive insolence.

"Stick your face in my hair one more time and see where it gets you. Is that, also, perfectly understood? Darling?"

Not waiting for a reply, she stood up, giving the stool a shove. It screeched against the polished floor, forcing him backward, startling him enough to let go of her.

She could have run at that moment, but she wasn't leaving without the diamond, and by the time she'd reached for it, Cyril had slipped an arm beneath her jacket. Kate felt the pressure of a blunt, unmistakable object forced against her back.

"No more of that," he said. "Do as I say, and do it quietly."

Bracing against a wave of panic, she fought to center herself in rage. She picked up the cigarette box and jeweler's case and put them in her purse.

"And your disguise," he murmured, nodding at the hat. "A poor one, but you look lovely in it. A shame to leave it behind."

She stuffed the hat into her purse as well, and allowed him to steer her away from the bar. They strolled up the crowded concourse at a casual, unhurried pace, acting the part of a reunited couple, with the level of their shoulders almost evenly matched.

"Since you know my name," Cyril said, "it seems only fair to tell me yours."

Apart from a reflexive desire to refuse it, she saw no point in withholding what he could find on the boarding passes in her purse. Kate surrendered her name, and he used it at once.

"Beautiful as you are, Kate, you are not the courier I expected."

"And you're not the Consul General I expected, so we're even. Phoebe described you, though, thinking you might be with him."

"Who are you, and why are you here, trying to disguise yourself as her?"

She had prepared for the possibility of this interaction and had her answers ready. "I wasn't *disguising* myself. I'm a courier with the Jewelers Security Alliance, licensed and insured. Phoebe is neither, which is why I'm here and she's not. She asked me to make this run for her. She tried reaching you at the Consulate to tell you but couldn't, and she didn't know who else to call."

"Interesting. My colleague at the Hotel Bonaventure didn't mention this switch. In fact, he never confirmed your arrival at all."

She shrugged. "I guess he didn't notice what I looked like. He seemed to be in a hurry, and since the instructions said I shouldn't talk to anyone, I didn't."

Cyril frowned and grew silent at this fabrication, but to Kate's relief he seemed to believe it. She looked at him from the corner of her eye. It may have been the grizzle in his cropped goatee, but he looked older than she'd expected. His large, round head was almost entirely bald, except for a circling band of gray stubble that made its domelike shape more noticeable. Like a man too conscious of his underaverage height, he walked with a stocky defiance, chest pushed forward so that his winter coat

—imitation cashmere, she spitefully noted—flopped open with each step.

As a physical specimen he looked far from invincible, but the point she'd scored and the grim pleasure she had taken in her head-butt had evaporated. Kate's courage had faltered with the first hard pressure against her back. She tried to retain a measure of anger, if only to keep her voice steady.

"Why did you need a courier at all? If you can smuggle a gun through airport security, why not a diamond?"

"How flattering you think me so clever," Cyril said, "but I have been cunning in a different way."

He left the statement hanging for a few paces, but no more than it took to pass the duty-free storefront. As she might have predicted, he couldn't resist the temptation to brag, which he did in the pedantic manner of a stage villain reciting his lines, carefully enunciating the longer words.

"You've heard of the auto-injector pen? Used to administer epinephrine, yes? A small modification made it ideal for my purpose. If your movements don't conform to my instructions, the solution is as easy as pulling a trigger. Once the device is armed, it's just a press of the thumb and the dose is delivered into your back."

"Something other than epinephrine, I assume," Kate said.

"Yes, something quite different. A tranquilizer dart, at the significant dosage we use on hyenas in the Sinai. The full effect is not instantaneous, but an appearance of intoxication begins almost immediately. I should warn you the device is armed, so we must be careful to avoid an accident. You would be unconscious in quite a short time."

"And what would you do with me, then?"

Cyril's chortling laugh had the wheezy character of a lifetime smoker, and his reply came in a more natural-sounding voice.

"Do you really want to find out?"

Probably not, Kate privately admitted, but wondered how much her prospects improved by following orders and staying awake.

You're trained and well able for it.

She'd been grateful for Conor's reassurance, but didn't feel very "able" right now. Like shuffling cards in a deck, she sifted through her training with MI6 the previous spring. Many lessons weren't applicable to her situation, and those that were seemed impossible to execute.

As though reading her mind, Cyril patted her arm with his free hand. "Please believe me, I don't wish to harm you, or anyone else. Think of it as something inconvenient that will soon be over."

"How soon?" Kate asked.

"Oh, three days at the most, and . . . yes. Number twenty-three. This is our gate."

She felt a cavern open inside her as they shuffled, still arm in arm, into the departure gate for the flight to Frankfurt. She'd only needed the boarding pass to access the international zone. Why had she duplicated Phoebe's instructions so exactly? She could have booked a flight to Paris, or London, or anywhere other than Frankfurt. Once Cyril had maneuvered them into side-by-side seats—the inseparable lovers bit was verging on farcical—he clarified it wouldn't have mattered anyway.

"You have a boarding pass for this flight, yes? If not, it doesn't matter. I booked the middle seat in our row as well to ensure privacy."

"Was this your plan for Phoebe, also?" Kate asked.

"Of course. A trip to Frankfurt, a short stay in a nice hotel, and a quick return home as soon as her knowledge of the diamond and its destination no longer mattered. I'm quite annoyed with Phoebe, now. She's made things more complicated for everyone. I'll call Becca to sort her out, but that's easiest done after I get you on board."

Becca.

It took a few seconds, but then Kate was back in the hushed, luxurious atmosphere of Harry Winston's VIP room, listening to Phoebe's trembling voice.

Becca swore me to secrecy and showed me the Star of the East.

The realization left her breathless. She and Conor had focused on Cyril and his possible infiltration of the Egyptian embassy, but all along it had been the Harry Winston manager in Buying and Sourcing who'd achieved a more impressive feat of espionage.

"Who's Becca?"

The question sounded strained and unnatural to her own ears, but Cyril appeared oblivious. He beamed at Kate.

"Really, it's Herebekka, her given Coptic name, but she prefers Becca now, and has trained me to remember it. I'll be meeting her in Alexandria tomorrow night. She's my daughter."

Chapter Forty-Four

CYRIL DIDN'T SEEM to notice Kate's flabbergasted silence, or that his words had packed such a wallop. His attention wandered to the flight crew members who were disappearing down the jet bridge to the plane, and she reminded herself that he couldn't realize how much she knew about the diamond and his plans for it.

She was still grappling with the surprise of this revelation when the speakers in the ceiling above them activated with a fizz of static. Next, she heard the boarding announcement for the flight to Frankfurt.

"Not long now, Kate." With one hand, Cyril reached for the leather carry-on he'd left on the floor between them and unzipped it. He nudged it in her direction with his foot. "The case, please."

She took it from her purse but didn't immediately put it in the carry-on. Kate held it on her lap, the soft, tawny leather yielding beneath her grip.

"I'd never seen anything like it," she said, her voice almost inaudible.

"Is that true?" Cyril looked amused. "Strange that a licensed and insured member of the Jewelers Security Alliance would be so awestruck."

The threat implied by the remark was clear. Once he had his

daughter on the phone, Becca would begin exploding Kate's story and digging into her background. How far could they go? How deep was their reach within the Egyptian embassy? And what did they intend to do about Phoebe, a loose end they would surely want snipped?

When she realized each question was only raising her fear to higher levels, Kate forced all of them from her mind. She put the case into the carry-on and zipped it, surprised her hands were so steady when her nerves felt ready to jump through her skin.

The gate attendant announced their zone, and once inside the plane, like a woman tumbling down a ravine, Kate groped for anything to hold on to, any avenue of escape.

"This isn't my seat assignment," she said when they reached Cyril's row. "My boarding pass says I should be—"

"Never mind. You are Phoebe, remember? Take hers." Cyril turned and gave her a gentle push toward the window seat, blocking her exit as he removed his coat. For the first time the pressure of his "cunning" auto-injector was gone from her back, leaving behind an isolated circle of pain. She got a glimpse of the device as he gingerly tucked the slender white tube up the sleeve of his sweater.

Cyril sat in the aisle seat and wedged the carry-on bag beneath the seat in front of him. He put his folded coat on the empty seat between them and smiled at her.

"We'll have a pleasant flight if you cooperate, or you can spend it sleeping."

Kate gave him a flat stare and turned away. She slumped down and faced the window, feigning compliance. From the minute they'd left the bar she'd been running escape sequences through her mind and had come close to launching one a few times, but in all of them she saw herself unconscious within minutes. Cyril needed only an instant to deploy his weapon.

If the injection was inevitable, Kate reasoned she could only hope to leverage the time available after it without looking like a messy drunk. Her best option—and probably, the last—would come soon. The flight attendants had seen her get on the plane sober, and any beverage service was a long way off. If she assembled and memorized her script now, and waited for the moment when the aisle was clear but the doors open—

"Excuse me? I think this is my seat."

Still facing the window, she lifted her head and turned to look for the source of the voice. A young woman with a mop of tangled brown curls stood in the aisle looking at her, squinting in apology, and Kate felt like she'd just seen an angel. It was a backpacker, one of those in the group at the Skyscapes bar.

"I knew you'd all be on this flight," she said.

The young woman charmed her with a confused, inebriated grin.

"I was on standby."

"I'm afraid you are mistaken, Miss," Cyril said briskly. "These seats are all taken."

"Oh. Weird." The backpacker frowned at her boarding pass. "Because, the lady at the gate—"

"Now how can I help out, here?"

With barely concealed excitement, Kate watched a well-groomed flight attendant with a Southern accent stride down the aisle, full of purpose. He had the forced brightness and matching smile of someone paid to care when no one is getting what they want. Plucking the boarding pass away from the young woman, he peered over his glasses at it.

"Sweetie, yes. This is your seat." With a flourish, he swept a hand over to Kate. "Ma'am, may I see your boarding pass please, and we'll get this fixed up?"

"But these seats are all taken," Cyril fumed. "I bought them myself."

"Well now, sir, this young lady cleared standby for 18A when the seat holder did not check in, and this young woman next to you has a boarding pass for 11D, and I see an empty seat there in the middle, so let's figure this out."

Recognizing a heaven-sent opening, Kate sailed through it.

"What a mess I've made. I guess I should have stayed in my own aisle, darling. We'll just shuffle around. She can have the window seat and I'll take the middle. Will that be all right?" She gave the flight attendant a full-wattage smile that he gratefully returned.

"Well that sounds just about perfect to me, and y'all can shuffle some more once we're airborne, if that'll help."

"No." Cyril tried again but was outflanked. Kate and her Southern hero were a team now.

"He's just tired," she said, with a private wink.

"And I know how that feels. Ma'am, I'm going to leave all this in your hands. You just let me know if I can do anything." With a parting wave, he sailed off down the aisle.

The young woman shifted the pack on her shoulder and inched forward, flattening herself against Cyril to make space for the last stragglers coming through. Stone-faced, he ignored her, staring straight ahead at the tray table in its locked, upright position. She looked at Kate with a helpless shrug.

"Come on, darling, you first." Full of loving indulgence, Kate prodded him. "I'm sure you don't want a scene."

At that, the stalemate fractured, as she knew it would. Two more people had now witnessed she was sober, fit, and lucid; he couldn't risk drawing the attention of everyone else. Cyril pulled at the seat in front of him and rose into the hunched posture of plane travelers everywhere. Whipping up the armrests, Kate picked up his coat, thrust it into his arms, and gave him a playful push into the aisle.

"We can't go through you, honey. Make some room."

She snatched up her purse and followed quickly, making it into the aisle with the backpack for cover, but as the young woman bent forward to toss it ahead into her seat, Cyril dropped his coat to the floor and grabbed Kate's wrist.

It came to her, then—the technique, the positioning, the motion and strength required. All of it. The right tool, and the perfect moment for it.

Making a hatchet of her hand, Kate slammed it against his forearm, a solid hit to the radial nerve. His arm dropped, and as the injector slid from his sleeve, she grabbed it, pressed it into his thigh, and hit the button.

Cyril stiffened in horror, his eyes widening. With a hint of anxiety Kate wondered if whatever was in the tube had been lethal, but then the reaction he'd promised began. His eyes drooped and turned glassy, his jaw loosened, and his tongue lolled.

As he struggled to speak, the effect grew more magnified. He sounded well and truly plastered.

"You *bitssh*," he hissed. "You fu-fuckinnng *bitssh*."

He made a fumbling attempt to grapple with her, drawing curious stares from the neighboring seats. His new seatmate in 18A, already wearing her earbuds, remained unaware.

"Ladies and gentlemen, the captain has asked us to close the cabin doors. We ask that you take your seats and prepare for departure, ensuring all personal items are securely stowed in the overhead compartments or beneath the seats in front of you."

Cyril's face contorted. The flight attendant's announcement seemed to flip a switch in his drowsy head. He lurched unsteadily, crashing back into his seat. Then, he rammed both feet forward, pushing the carry-on bag with the jeweler's case farther beneath the one in front of him.

Kate stared at his legs, locked and rigid. She bit her lip, and ran for the door.

Chapter Forty-Five

ALTHOUGH THE ENTIRE point of a "burner phone" was to use it only once, Conor had continued his unbroken streak of poor cell phone management by giving Kate the number to the one he'd used to call Frank. Given his history, she hit the speed dial button with low expectations while in a dead sprint from the international departures zone. Miraculously, he answered on the first ring and barked a question at her in place of a greeting.

"Are you okay?"

"Yes. I'm fine," she said, panting. She dodged a luggage trolley and headed toward the concourse wall where traffic was thinner.

"You don't sound fine. What's wrong?"

"What's wrong is my plane is leaving, and I'm not on it yet."

"For the love of Christ, Kate." Relief, exasperation, and amusement combined in Conor's voice. "It's nearly half six. What the hell has been going on?"

"I can't talk fast enough to tell you, now, but you need to find Phoebe. I think she's in danger."

"Are *you* in danger?"

"No!"

"Then why is she?"

"No. Time." Kate cornered a turn and saw the security check-in for the transborder zone at the end of the corridor.

"He'll be unconscious soon, but he might have time for a phone call, and if he gets through, Becca will be looking for her."

"Who is unconscious? What does Becca—wait, *Becca?*"

"Conor, stop asking questions! Phoebe said she'd be at the salon until eight tonight, so try there, first. If she's not there, you can—"

"Right, right, okay, I know how to trace people, thanks very much. I'll find her. Are you going to make the flight? That's a question. Sorry."

Kate grinned. "I am *absolutely* going to make this flight."

A minute longer would have proved her a liar, but she skidded up to the gate just as the door was closing and did the walk of shame down the aisle, ignoring the glares trained on her. Half the seats were empty and she had a row to herself.

"I didn't even have to buy them all."

She took the seat next to the window, and as if to reinforce how close she'd come to being left behind, the plane started backing away from the terminal.

Kate brushed a trickle of sweat from her temple and popped open her purse. Then, she flipped up the cover of the Marlboro box, and she and the Star of the East winked at each other.

Chapter Forty-Six

COMPARED to its more famous neighbor less than a hundred yards away, the Pierre Hotel kept a low profile on its corner at Central Park South. It couldn't compete with the scale or notoriety of the Plaza, nor did it try. Confident of its own brand of luxury, the Pierre disdained comparisons, and Conor had to admit it had earned the right to that self-esteem.

He'd been prepared to find its opulence off-putting, but it was hard not to be struck by the beauty of its interior; and the pride and affection for the hotel shown by every staff member he encountered won him over.

Choosing to believe in Kate's optimism, he'd brought her suitcase and garment bag from Sophia's apartment and booked a room to give her a place to change. After tipping a bellhop to deliver the luggage, he'd hurried up to the second floor, where Douglas Chatham's holiday party was hitting its stride.

The bar had a room to itself, and it was an impressive one. The Rotunda Foyer leading to the Cotillion Ballroom had a double-sided marble staircase curving down into an ornate, oval space that might have been transported from a French château. Surrounding murals featured mythological figures striking poses on a background of leafy trees and blue sky, a theme that continued in the cloud-and-sky-painted ceiling.

The room's candelabra sconces were dimmed to create a twilight scene, but it allowed enough light for Conor, who'd been killing time for the past hour, to inspect the more lighthearted figures painted on the walls. One of them bore a striking resemblance to Jackie Kennedy.

He'd spoken with Kate when she'd arrived at LaGuardia, but the conversation had been mostly one-sided as the signal inside the hotel kept fading. From her, Conor gathered enough to alert Frank that United Flight 89 from Montreal would reach Frankfurt airport in four hours carrying a Coptic revolutionary who might not be awake when the plane landed. For his part, he'd been able to communicate only that Phoebe was safe, with details to come, and that there was a room key waiting for Kate at the front desk.

She'd phoned again from the room an hour later. The Star of the East was in the hotel manager's vault, she was getting dressed, and Conor should stay where he was. Hearing sounds of stiletto heels hitting the floor and makeup gear clattering onto the sink's counter, he was happy to follow instructions.

He drifted back to the Cotillion Ballroom, stepping into a festive, winter wonderland theme lit with a moonlight glow. Two central buffets anchored the room, topped by tall, frosted trees, their branches twinkling with fairy lights and decked with strings of crystal. A four-piece jazz ensemble played on a low stage at one end. Light-projected snowflakes floated over the parquet dance floor in front of them.

As he entered, a group of strangers turned to him with theatrical smiles of delight baffling Conor until he realized the target of their excitement was behind him. He'd come in a few steps ahead of Douglas Chatham and his wife, Anna. It was typical of the man's egotism to arrive late for a party he was hosting himself.

"Hey! Conor!" Kate's father grabbed his hand and thumped him on the shoulder. "Have any run-ins with hunters lately?"

"How are you, Douglas," Conor said, reciprocating the

crushing handshake. "Sure you'd be surprised. You can't swing a cat in Vermont without clipping a hunter. Anna, you're looking lovely as ever."

Kate's stepmother was a timid runway model with wide, perpetually startled eyes and a personality that seemed concentrated in her honey-blond hair. It had been shoulder-length when he'd seen her over the summer, but now it looked like a barber had taken a run at her. A number four cut, Conor estimated.

He gave her a cautious peck on the cheek, getting a whispery smile and an air kiss in return. She made him think of Venetian glass, something thin and decorative, and too easily shattered.

"Where's Katie?" Douglas was already looking past Conor to wave and point at his guests, showing a mouth full of blinding white teeth.

"I'm expecting her any minute. She's just upstairs, ehm . . . adjusting her finery."

"Aha! Booked a room? Didn't realize it."

"It's more of a staging area, I suppose," Conor admitted.

"Super!"

His approval was so emphatic Conor felt he'd scored a point simply by paying a small fortune for a changing room. His future father-in-law gave him another clout on the shoulder before moving off with Anna, disappearing into a throng of admirers.

After a glance at his watch, he headed for the buffet table. He loaded a plate with smoked salmon canapés, prosciutto and melon, cocktail shrimp, something mysterious in puff pastry, and a few chicken skewers. When he turned around, Kate was standing in front of him and Conor nearly dropped everything on the floor.

She wore a strapless gown in burgundy-colored satin, with a slit up the side. A necklace of emeralds and rubies edged in gold circled her neck, matched with a set of drop earrings.

"Hand it over," she said, nodding at the plate. "I've had nothing but two Bavarian cookies today, and the sugar rush is long gone."

Conor smiled. "I got it for you, anyway. Let me know what I should stay away from. My God, Kate, you look . . ."

He trailed off, his glib Irish tongue failing him for once.

Aware of the attention of those around them, she cupped the back of his neck and gave him a chaste but lingering kiss on the cheek.

"You, too. The way a tux looks on you should be against the law."

Conor gave her a napkin and brandished the plate like a butler with a tray. As he expected, she zeroed in on the smoked salmon.

"Thank you, my dear." Kate popped the canapé in her mouth and briefly closed her eyes. "Now, I have breaking news. I briefed Agent Toomey as soon as I landed, and he called me a few minutes ago. He and Agent Knox are going to come for the diamond in the morning, but the more exciting update is they found Becca's name on the manifest for a flight leaving tonight from JFK to Alexandria. The pilot got pulled back to the gate before takeoff, and two US Marshals took her off the plane in handcuffs."

"That's brilliant! Score one for Reid's team," Conor said. "He'll be chuffed."

"Did he have his surgery?" Kate asked.

"It's tomorrow morning. I told him we'd come round his room in the afternoon." He accepted a shot glass of gazpacho from a passing tray. "As it happens, I have a pretty big piece of news, as well. It turns out the Star of the East doesn't belong to the Egyptian government at all."

Chapter Forty-Seven

KATE SPAT a sip of wine back into her glass. "I was *not* ready for that one. Are you kidding me?"

"See that woman behind me, in the dress with all the bows on, and the man with her? That's Jeff and Marion Winston," Conor said. "Sophia introduced me; they're friends of hers."

"Oh, of course! Harry's nephew. She mentioned them to me this morning. I guess Daddy connected him with an investor at one of these parties. Jeff knew something about the diamond?"

"Yup. He said his uncle sold it to a private collector about ten years before he died, but in 1984 the Harry Winston company bought it back, and they've had it ever since."

"This had nothing to do with the Egyptian embassy at all, then? It was a straight-up jewel heist concocted between Cyril and his daughter?"

"Correct, but all in aid of the larger cause against Mubarak, and the protection of the Coptic community. When I phoned Frank, telling him to get someone over to Frankfurt Airport, he had an update as well. MI6 has connected Cyril to the lieutenant-general they're listening to in Cairo. Also, the Canadians reported Mounir has cracked wide open. Turns out he's been transferring trunkloads of cash on the Hollumborg for the past year, and they've been using it to sweeten up the generals for . . . what's wrong?"

While Conor talked, Kate had been steadily emptying the plate of hors d'oeuvres he still held for her, but now, looking troubled, she returned the square of prosciutto-wrapped melon she'd lifted from it.

"I can't help second guessing the choices we've made," she said. "This group is trying to protect their own community in a popular revolt against a dictator, and we just made it harder for them. Nobody had seen that diamond for years. Who knows how long it would have taken for anyone to miss it. I wonder if we should have let them have it."

"I don't think you believe that."

"I suppose not." Kate sighed. "But, I'd like to feel more confident we chose the right side in all this."

"We may never be sure what side we even landed on," Conor said. "If there's one thing I've learned about this game, it's that there are always new webs getting woven inside the old ones. MI6 is going to want a long chat with Cyril, but don't assume that means they'll blow the whistle on him."

"Really? Do you think they might decide to help him?"

"I wouldn't bet against it, but who knows?" He skewered the melon and held it out to her. "Maybe we'll turn on the news someday and find out."

Kate leaned forward, delicately took the melon into her mouth, and left him holding the toothpick. Conor sketched an accusatory baton gesture at her before dropping it on the plate.

"You know what that dress is doing to me, and you're enjoying it far too much. That reminds me—Jeff Winston knows Becca, as well. I slipped her into the conversation, and he implied she got her job at Buying and Sourcing because she's sleeping with one of the corporate directors. He says she's quite a stunner."

"I wonder why—" Before Kate could go on, some of her college girlfriends interrupted them, eager for details about the wedding plans.

Conor had met this group of friends the previous winter when they'd spent a weekend at the inn. They were intelligent, warm, and genuine, and he'd liked all of them. Kate kept a firm grip on his hand, as if afraid he might bolt while they gushed over the news about Jamaica, but he wasn't tempted.

He liked seeing this side of her personality, laughing and clowning with her mates, and he especially enjoyed watching her tonight. What would her friends think, he wondered, if they knew only hours ago she'd outsmarted a thief, escaped him using a radial nerve strike, and prevented a historic and priceless gem from being lost forever? He imagined they'd be as awestruck as he was.

After the group drifted off for fresh drinks from the bar, Kate pulled him over to a quiet corner and took up the conversation where they'd left it.

"I was just wondering why Becca—oh, my God! Conor, am I hallucinating, or is that Phoebe over there talking to my brother?"

"Well spotted. That's herself, and that is indeed Peter." Conor grinned. He'd been waiting for her to notice. "I'd no time to organize anything on the fly, so we picked her up on the way to the party."

"*We?*" Kate gaped at him. "You're not telling me you brought my grandmother to the Harry Winston salon with you?"

"Well, technically it was Rocco who brought us both."

"Who the hell is Rocco?!"

"Sophia's driver. Did you not meet him this morning? Nice bloke. What's so funny?"

"Never mind. Go on, please."

"Right."

Conor offered Kate the last of the hors d'oeuvres—the puff pastry with the mystery filling—which she declined. He ate it himself, brightening when it turned out to be a bit of shredded, barbecued beef, then slid the empty plate onto a passing banquet tray that was full of them.

"Anyway, no," he said. "I didn't bring your grandmother into the salon. Rocco and Sophia sat on a side street with the car running, and I legged it inside. There was a nasty piece of work at the door who couldn't be arsed with me, nor I with her. I was busting ahead on my own when she got the security guard on to me, but he was no bother. I came out with something about a family emergency and he brought me right round to Phoebe's office."

Conor paused, laughing a little as he remembered the encounter. "She's quite a nervous bird, isn't she? There I was, looking perfectly civilized in my tux, but she nearly disappeared under the feckin' desk before I could say a word. I hadn't much to say, anyway, because you hadn't told me what was going on, but between the two of us we pieced it together. My biggest question was why Becca didn't keep it simple and take the diamond herself, since she had access to it."

"That's exactly what I was wondering," Kate said.

"Well, it comes down to paperwork. Phoebe says nobody, not even the CEO, can get at her special set of keys and remove something from the vault without a raft of paperwork. I think Becca was a fairly bloody-minded daughter, happy to use her father's signature and his embassy credentials on the forms. It meant if anything went wrong, she could buy herself some time to escape while the blame got pinned on him."

Conor swiveled to look at Phoebe, who was still in deep conversation with Kate's brother near the dance floor. "Hashing through all that with her didn't help the nerves at all, but I hustled her out to the car, and then got a few drinks into her once we arrived here. Peter's been latched on to her ever since, and she seems to be enjoying it, so I'd say it's fair odds she'll turn up at our wedding."

He felt Kate lean against him. Circling her waist, Conor looked anxiously at her, and relaxed when he saw she was laughing.

"I can't wait to hear what kind of spin you put on all this for Oma," she said.

"Ah. Well. I didn't, in fact, spin it."

"What?" She pulled away to look at him, a tentative hope flickering over her face.

He nodded. "It was the right thing to do. She deserves the

truth, which you already knew, of course. I've promised between the two of us she'll get the full story before we go home. . . ."

He trailed off as Kate's eyes filled. Even knowing they were happy tears it was almost more than he could stand.

"I didn't think it was possible for me to love you more, Conor McBride. Somehow, you keep surprising me."

"It should have happened sooner, I realize that now, and I'm sorry. I just—"

Her sudden, ardent kiss prevented any further expression of regret. He yielded to it, allowing himself to forget they were in a room with a hundred and seventy-five people, almost all of them strangers to him.

"It's the best Christmas gift you could have given me," she said, as they separated, slowly, reluctantly.

"I'll be honest, though," Conor murmured, giving her lower lip another caress. "I'm nearly smothered with the fear of how she'll take it."

"Don't underestimate her," Kate said. "She survived the Nazis, remember. This won't be much of a challenge for her."

"That's a fair point."

Looking over her shoulder, he saw the woman herself, as if conjured from the air at that very moment. Standing within a foot of them, Sophia was holding two glasses of Champagne in exquisitely carved flutes. From her smile it was clear the public display of affection had her approval. It was also clear they had attracted the attention of everyone in the room.

Chapter Forty-Eight

WITH A WHISPER, Conor turned Kate to face her grandmother while taking a quick read of the room. Everyone looking at them had their own glass of Champagne, and Douglas Chatham was onstage, conferring with a member of the jazz ensemble. The formal part of the evening's agenda was about to begin.

"Your father is getting ready to propose a toast," Sophia said to Kate, offering the glasses.

"Oh!"

After this single exclamation, Kate's embarrassment left her incapable of further speech or movement. Conor watched the blush rise over her skin. From the décolletage of her dress, it spread up her neck and out to her ears. Holding back a grin, he stepped forward to accept the glasses from Sophia with a wink.

"We'll be ready." He handed a glass to Kate and looked at his own. "Hang on, this is Galway crystal, isn't it?"

Sophia looked delighted. "I'm so pleased you recognize it. I had them custom-made for the two of you."

With a subtle pressure, Conor stepped on Kate's toe, which produced the desired effect. She came to life again with a quick smile and kissed her grandmother, once on each cheek.

"Thank you so much, Oma. They're gorgeous."

Kate's father was now giving a few imperious taps on the microphone. In commiseration with the musicians, Conor winced at the echoing *thunk* it sent through the ballroom. It proved an effective signal for everyone to fasten their eyes on the stage, and in particular, on Douglas Chatham, who soaked in the attention like it was a life-giving sun.

"What a great evening! It's always a good time, isn't it?" he began, and continued along the same line for several minutes, warming up his audience with remarks guaranteed to produce applause. When he finally worked his way to what seemed like the start of a formal toast, Douglas kept some of the spotlight for himself, in a way that made Conor wish there'd been time to throw down a whiskey or two before he'd started.

"Along with the usual holiday fun, which we'll get back to soon, I also wanted to take the opportunity to announce that Kate, my youngest daughter, is getting married again. I think some of you were at the first wedding, at our place on one of the Thimble Islands up on Long Island Sound. Beautiful spot."

Feeling Kate go rigid next to him, Conor slipped an arm around her and saw the high color of just a moment earlier drain from her face as quickly as it came.

"Kate?"

"I'm okay," she whispered, and then added, "for now."

Just as Conor became convinced he'd begin life with his father-in-law by putting the man in the hospital, Douglas seemed to sense the awkward restlessness of his guests, if not the cause of it, and hurried on with the formalities of the toast.

"Anyway, the next one is going to be bigger and better. I'll be seeing most of you again this spring, down in Jamaica, when Katherine Chatham weds Conor McBride, over there." He made a waving motion in Conor's direction. "Super guy, Conor. Straight from the Emerald Isle. Amazing fiddle player. So, let's raise our glasses for a Cristal toast to the handsome couple. Nothing but the best for my baby girl."

Conor turned to Kate. Relieved to see her calm expression, he tapped the beautiful Galway-crafted glass against hers, and they drained them in unison.

"I need something a lot stronger," she said, after their showy, Champagne-flavored kiss had satisfied the crowd.

"So do I," Sophia said, taking the flutes and tucking them back into a velvet-lined box. The three of them looked at each other and laughed.

"I'll winch a bottle away from the bartender," Conor said, watching a member of the jazz ensemble approach the microphone. "In a minute or two, though. I don't think we've finished the program yet."

"Ladies and gentlemen, we've got a great dance set coming up for you, but before that gets started, I'm going to ask Conor and Kate to lead it off with an engagement dance to a special little tune."

"Oh my God." Kate spun around to Conor with transparent alarm, fearful of a reaction she might prevent if she caught it soon enough. "Conor, I promise you, I had no idea he would do this. It wasn't in any program notes that I ever saw."

Looking at her, Conor felt his heart soar and sink in the same moment. The lift told him how much he loved her, and the fall proved what an ass he'd been, about things that mattered only if he gave them the power to affect him.

"It's all right, love." He held out a hand to her. "It wasn't him; it was me."

Even in a state of utter confusion, Kate trusted him. She took his hand and followed him onto the dance floor.

"I don't understand. What do you mean, it was you?"

"The music was the only part of the agenda I could influence, so I did." He lifted her hand and she followed his lead, pirouetting on the snowflake-strewn parquet before settling into his arms.

"Did you not notice the violinist?" Conor said, with a nod at the woman who was taking up her position next to the piano. "I booked the band, and the tune she mentioned is one I wrote for you. At first, I thought I'd play it for you myself, but then it seemed a nicer idea to dance to it."

"I don't . . . wait. What?"

Conor felt all the nervous tension in her body release.

"You're saying you wrote the song they're going to play? For me?"

"That's exactly what I'm saying. Hush, now. It's starting."

He took a deep breath as the opening piano notes began. He was nervous, as well. It wasn't the first piece he'd ever written, but it was the only one he'd turned over to someone else for a performance he was hearing for the first time himself. He worried about what a jazz musician would make of a traditional, quintessentially Celtic air. With the first notes of the solo violinist, Conor knew it was all fine. The musician understood what he was trying to say. She'd captured it.

He wasn't a spectacular dancer, but an adequate one, and Kate had recovered enough to follow the waltz-like rhythm of the music. They danced as if the room were empty, with delicate ornamentations of sound floating around them, and tears streaming down her cheeks.

"Does it have a name?" Kate asked.

"I'd been still working on it a few days ago, so I hadn't really settled on one," Conor said. "Listening to it now, though, it feels like I should stay with what I've been calling it in my head for the past six months: *Kate's Grace Notes.*"

"You finished it only a few days ago?"

"It will never really be finished. I can go on forever with grace notes. Especially yours."

Conor twirled her around to face the guests who had gathered around the dance floor, and caught sight of Douglas standing at its corner, wearing the bemused expression of someone moved by a feeling he doesn't understand.

"Look at your poor Da," he said. "He doesn't know where he's at."

Kate laughed. "And you love that."

"I love *you*."

"I love you back. Something fierce."

Running a finger lightly along her skin, Conor traced the line of her sparkling emerald necklace, making her shiver.

"Sorry," he said, his voice strained and husky.

"Don't be. That was a good shiver." Kate rested her head against his shoulder. "Conor?"

"Hmm?"

"Let's keep the hotel room for the night."

"Good idea."

"And let's go up to it soon."

Conor kissed her, ignoring her father, her grandmother, and every other curious eye around him. As it turned out, he was having an excellent night.

About the Author

Author of the award-winning Conor McBride International Mystery Series, Kathryn Guare's character-driven novels are a mix of page-turning suspense and travel adventure, balanced with a little romance and humor. She has a passion for exploring diverse cultures and cuisine, Classical music, and all things Celtic, and mixes these into her stories along with other enthusiasms that capture her imagination. Formerly, as an executive with a global health advocacy organization, she traveled extensively throughout the world. Currently, as a native Vermonter, she hates to leave home during foliage season.

For news on upcoming books:
KATHRYNGUARE.COM

facebook.com/KathrynGuare

amazon.com/author/kathrynguare

instagram.com/kguare

pinterest.com/kguare1

twitter.com/KGuare

bookbub.com/authors/kathryn-guare

www.ingramcontent.com/pod-product-compliance
Lightning Source LLC
Chambersburg PA
CBHW010547100726
47902CB00008B/2109